'That's my boy. Give it to Daddy.'

Kieran gasped. 'What did you say?'

The air whooshed out of her lungs. Where had that come from? She'd intended discussing with Kieran what she should call him when talking to Seamus *before* she mentioned the D word. She stared at Kieran, aghast. He looked as shocked as she felt. 'I'm sorry. I shouldn't have said that. I—'

She spun around to the bench, staring at her shaking hands as she tried to pick up a knife to slice the tomatoes. He'd never talk to her again. At least not for the rest of the night—if he stayed now.

'Abby, it's all right.' Kieran's hand touched her shoulder, pressured her to turn to face him. 'I should have a name, and I guess I *am* Seamus' father.'

Seamus bumped between their legs, startling them both into looking down. He held the opener up to Kieran.

Shock drained the colour from Kieran's cheeks. 'Did he really understand you? Does he know I'm his father?'

Kieran stared at his son, speechless. Then slowly he crouched down and took the opener in one hand. He ran the other hand over Seamus' head, and whispered, 'Thanks, boyo.'

Dear Reader

Sunny Nelson is truly one of New Zealand's gems. I moved there eighteen years ago and instantly felt at home. The city is small, but vibrant. It is picturesque, with a harbour at the front door and mountains in the background. I learnt to fly at Nelson's airport—the one mentioned in this book. Hope does exist, and I have regularly bought fruit at the orchards lining the roads. I met my husband in Nelson, so for me it is the perfect setting for a romance.

Abby and Kieran have a lot to overcome when they come together. But they both have so much to give to each other—and to little Olivia and Seamus—that they can't go wrong. If only they can put the past behind them…

I hope you enjoy following their journey as they move forward to a rewarding and loving life together.

Cheers!

Sue MacKay
www.suemackay.nz.co

PLAYBOY DOCTOR TO DOTING DAD

BY
SUE MacKAY

First published in Great Britain 2011
by Mills & Boon,
an imprint of Harlequin (UK) Limited,
Large Print edition 2011
Eton House, 18-24 Paradise Road,
Richmond, Surrey TW9 1SR   **11774628**

© Sue MacKay 2011

ISBN: 978 0 263 21763 6

Printed and bound in Great Britain
by CPI Antony Rowe, Chippenham, Wiltshire

With a background working in medical laboratories, and a love of the romance genre, it is no surprise that **Sue MacKay** writes Medical™ Romance stories. An avid reader all her life, she wrote her first story at age eight—about a prince, of course. She lives with her husband in beautiful Marlborough Sounds, at the top of New Zealand's South Island, where she can indulge her passions for the outdoors, the sea and cycling. She is currently training as a volunteer ambulance officer.

A recent title by the same author:

THEIR MARRIAGE MIRACLE

To Louise Groarke,
my wonderful critique partner.

And to Iona Jones, Barb Jeffcott Geris,
Margie Stewart, Deborah Shattock and
Emily Gee—of the very supportive
Blenheim Writers group.

CHAPTER ONE

ABBY BROWN stared out of the window at the long, neat rows of nectarine trees with their small fruit that were just beginning to fill out. Her father's orchard: the one constant in her life. Each season brought its own routine and, with summer officially starting this week, December meant spraying and crop thinning.

Stop procrastinating. This had to be done. On a long, indrawn breath, she pressed redial. The one phone call she did not want to make, had tried making for two years. She knew the number off by heart she'd rung it so often. But this time she actually had to let the phone ring. Had to wait for Kieran to answer. This time she could not hang up in a panic. She could no longer put off telling him.

This was her third attempt to reach him to-night, and the only reason she kept trying was because having this particular conversation face to face with him would be worse. A whole lot worse.

The ringing stopped as the phone was picked up somewhere in Dublin. 'Kieran Flynn speaking.'

Words died on Abby's tongue. That sweet Irish lilt reminded her exactly why she'd got into this situation in the first place.

'Hello? Anyone there?' Kieran asked, a smile in his voice.

She couldn't do this.

She had to do it. Quickly, before she could slam the phone down, she answered, 'It's Abby Brown.'

'Abigail? Really? Where are you? I mean, are you here? Or are you calling from New Zealand?' Measured surprise lifted his voice.

'I'm at home.' How could she afford to travel to Ireland? 'I thought it was about time I made contact with you.'

'What a coincidence. I'm coming down your way in a few days.' Kieran paused then added, 'I'm working in your local hospital for two months, managing the emergency department.'

'I heard. The hospital grapevine is in good

working order. I had hoped you'd have been in touch before coming out.'

'I thought I'd wait until I'd settled in, get to know my way around first, before giving you a call. I also wondered if I might possibly spend some time with Olivia.'

Yeah, sure. His niece. The little girl they had joint guardianship of. The child he barely remembered to send birthday and Christmas presents to. Had he really intended calling? Or did he think this was the right thing to say now that she'd contacted him? Obviously he hadn't realised he'd see her at the hospital. Heaven help her. It wasn't going to be easy if they didn't get past the news she had for him. 'We'll be working together.'

'We will? That's fantastic. For some reason I thought you were nursing in Paediatrics.' Charm thickened the lilt.

It also sent the muscles in her stomach into spasms, which was plain stupid because she didn't hold any special feelings for this man. Really? 'I transferred to ED nearly a year ago. I prefer it to Paediatrics.' These days she didn't like dealing with sick children all the time. It made her worry too much. At least in ED she worked with a variety of patients.

'Then we'll have plenty of time to see each other, and catch up on things. Should be fun.'

Things? A child was not a thing. 'That will be great. Olivia needs to get to know her Irish family.'

'I guess so.' He sounded unsure. Backing off already?

'Of course she does. It's an important part of her heritage. I think I'm right in believing you're the only living relative on her mother's side.'

'No, there is her grandfather, but I haven't a clue where he is these days. I don't think there's any hurry for Olivia to meet him. In fact, she's probably a whole lot better off never knowing him.'

'That's kind of sad.' She couldn't imagine not knowing where her father was, or any member of her family for that matter. 'Olivia adores her Kiwi grandfather.'

'Then she's very lucky and we should leave the situation as it stands.' His tone suggested she'd be wise not to argue.

Okay, so she could be patient, give him time to get to know Olivia better before raising the point again. But right now she was being side-tracked from the purpose of this call. Again a deep breath.

But Kieran spoke before she could gather the courage to tell him.

'Look, Abigail, I hate to rush you but I've got lots to do before I catch my plane out. Two months is a long time to be away from my job here. Did you ring for a specific reason? Or is this a welcoming call before I arrive in Nelson?'

Here it was, the moment she'd been dreading. 'I have to tell you something that I think it best you know before you get here.' Before she saw him again, and read the shock and anger that would surely fill those startling blue eyes that haunted her every day. Tell him, get it over. 'I have a son, Seamus. He's fifteen months old.' The words poured out in a torrent, her mouth dry.

'Oh, right. A playmate for Olivia, then. That must be good for her.'

He paused, and Abby waited, her stomach in a knot, her heart thumping in her chest.

Then she gasped, surprising hurt spiralling through her, when he said, 'Of course, I didn't know you were in a relationship. Have you married since we last saw each other?'

Didn't he get it? Come on, Kieran. Do the sum. Fifteen months plus nine? What had they been doing together two years ago? Had he forgotten that night they'd spent making love? A night that had never faded completely from her memory. But, then, he didn't have a young child running around his home to constantly remind him of that time, so he probably had forgotten. Strange how disappointed that made her feel.

She blurted, 'Seamus is your son.'

There, she'd told him. She couldn't take the words back. The truth was out. And the silence was deafening. Of course she'd been wrong not to have told him the moment she'd seen the blue line on the pregnancy testing strip. But his career was very demanding and he'd been afraid of having anything to do with Olivia. He'd told Abby bluntly that he believed the child would come a distant second to his job. He'd warned he'd probably send Olivia to boarding school as soon as she was old enough. Providing financial backing seemed to be his share of the guardianship issue. And Olivia was only his niece. What chance was there that he'd go the extra

distance for their son? So Abby, concerned about
the emotional damage Kieran believed he was
capable of inflicting, had taken the easy option
and kept quiet.

Huh. Easy? That'd be the day. She'd agonised
over her decision every single day, knowing
Kieran should be told about his child. All those
aborted phone calls she'd made to him. And then
there were the many letters she'd written and not
posted. The photos of Seamus she'd taken and
not sent. None of that counted for anything now.

'Kieran?' she finally whispered.

'Are you sure he's mine?' The charm had disappeared now, replaced by uncertainty.

Thanks a bunch. 'I don't make a habit of sleeping around.' But she had spent one passionate
night with this man, a night that had been totally out of character for her. She'd been numb
with grief for her brother and sister-in-law, and
Kieran's arms had been warm and comforting.
Too comforting.

He continued, 'What I meant was I used pre-
cautions each time.'

'Ah, well, there was once when, um, we kind
of forgot.'

'I never forget. The last thing I have ever

wanted is to be a parent. Because of that I make doubly sure something like this won't happen. Ever.' His voice snapped out that last word.

Sorry, buddy. I've got the evidence. 'Seamus is the spitting image of you. Your colouring, that slight lift of the right side of your mouth when you smile. I wouldn't be surprised if, when he starts talking, he has an Irish accent.'

Again silence fell between them. Abby twisted her hair around her fingers as she stared outside. Dusk was falling, softening the view. She'd told Kieran. At last. Even if he exploded at her, called her every miserable name he could think of, she felt as though a huge weight had finally been lifted. Not telling Kieran about Seamus had never sat comfortably with her. She mightn't trust him to do the right thing by his child, or by her. She might believe he'd back out of their lives so fast he'd be like a train without brakes; but it went against all she believed in not to have told him the truth. Sound reasons or not.

'Am I to understand that you're only telling me now because I'm coming out to Nelson this week?'

'Yes.' She waited for the explosion, shoulders

tense, fingers white where they gripped the phone.

'There's an honest answer.' Were his teeth grinding? 'Why didn't you tell me the moment you knew you were pregnant?'

'What would you have done about it, if I had?'

'How do I know? I haven't got a clue what to say now, so as to what I'd have said or done two years ago is beyond me. But I would've had time to get used to the idea.' He didn't sound like he'd really grasped what she'd told him. As in really, truly, understood that he had a child. Too much to take in?

She tried to explain the inexcusable. 'You had made it abundantly clear how you felt about having a child of your own.' On two occasions. 'I'm talking about your reaction to becoming Olivia's guardian. You were so adamant you didn't want anything to do with her upbringing that I…' She faltered. 'I figured if you couldn't cope with helping bring up your niece, the last thing you'd want to deal with would be a child of your own.' Don't forget the financial side. 'I know you've provided well for Olivia, very well, but I didn't want you to think I was asking for that for Seamus.'

'That gave you the right to decide I shouldn't know about this boy? My son?' His words were like bullets, slamming into her with piercing sharpness. 'You made this choice? For me?'

She would not apologise. She'd seen the trepidation clouding his eyes at the thought that he might have to raise Olivia. Trepidation that in truth she'd never fully understood. Had she done the guy an injustice? Probably. The guilt twisted her gut. But what hope was there that he'd have been willing to become a father to Seamus? In his own words, no father at all was better than a random one, and he'd told her they didn't come more random than he'd be. 'Kieran, rightly or wrongly, I had my reasons. But now that you're coming here, you need to know.' Hopefully he'd have calmed down by the time she got to see him at work. 'And I want Seamus to know his father.'

There was a sharp intake of breath at the other end of the line. Had she gone too far?

If so, he didn't divulge his feelings. 'I won't have much spare time during my tenure at your hospital, so I hope you're not expecting a lot from me.'

Only some time with your niece, who really needs to get to know her mother's brother. Only an acknowledgement of your son, and maybe a softening of your heart towards him. Only your understanding and forgiveness. Too much to expect? Probably.

He continued, 'Spare time or not, we have a lot to discuss. I'll set up a meeting with you once I've settled in.'

Set up a meeting? Her shoulders slumped. That's not the way to go about this. But she'd leave it for now. 'I'm sorry you had to find out this way, Kieran.'

What happened to not apologising? The trouble with that notion was that she felt incredibly guilty. Not only had Kieran missed out on so much of his son's life, if he'd wanted to be a part of it, but Seamus had also missed out on too much. And right at this moment she suspected Seamus would continue losing out for a very long time to come. Maybe, when he was an adult, he'd be able to approach his father and see if they could establish a bond.

Unless she could patch things up with Kieran. She didn't like her chances.

Five days later

Abby blinked. Nelson Airport terminal already? It seemed only moments ago she'd pulled out of the hospital car park. Had she been speeding? Not when she didn't want to be here, surely? Not even running ten minutes late would've made her speed today. Meeting Kieran Flynn was right at the bottom of her 'want-to-do' list. Right there after going to the dentist.

But he'd emailed to ask, no, demand, that she meet his flight. Michael, the department head Kieran was temporarily replacing, had thought it an excellent idea. 'A friendly gesture,' he'd said. So why hadn't Michael thought of meeting the man? And saved her the anguish of being squeezed inside her car with a hostile Irishman?

She stopped her old Nissan Bluebird in the two-minute pick-up zone and shoved out into the searing mid-afternoon heat that not even the offshore breeze helped to cool. Her skin instantly prickled with perspiration as she slung her handbag over her shoulder. Sucking in her churning stomach, she locked the car door, all the while fighting the urge to leap back in and race away.

Gritting her teeth, she headed for the main

entrance. As her sandals slapped the hot, sticky pavement she practised a welcoming smile. And failed. Miserably.

Today she would have to face Kieran for the first since telling him he was a father. The ramifications of what she'd done, or not done, were about to start. She'd thought the hardest part had been phoning him the other day, but now she had to actually see him. No doubt he'd have spent the thirty-plus hours flying to New Zealand, thinking up truckloads of horrible things to say to her. Unfortunately, she knew she probably deserved them.

The yoghurt she'd eaten for lunch curdled in her stomach and her mouth soured. She hesitated. It would be so easy to turn around and head back to work, bury herself in broken bones and chest pains.

Merely delaying tactics. Kieran would still catch up with her.

Dragging her feet through the main doors, her eyes scanned the noisy crowd for the tall, dark-haired Irishman who'd haunted her dreams for the past two years. No sign of him. A wave of relief engulfed her. Maybe he wasn't coming? Maybe he'd changed his mind.

But common sense prevailed. Of course he hadn't changed his mind. He'd made a commitment to the hospital and if she knew one thing about Kieran Flynn, it was that he didn't break commitments. Especially when they involved his work. But a commitment to a child? He hadn't broken one to Olivia because he'd never made one. Abby knew that Kieran's strong belief that he'd be an inadequate father had been behind his decision not to be a part of Olivia's upbringing. And behind her own decision not to tell him about Seamus. She rubbed a hand down her cheek as she remember the slap of his hand on the lawyer's desk as he had stated categorically that she should never expect him to be there for Olivia in any role other than a distant uncle who'd finance the child's education. Abby now realised that she needed to learn more about what was behind this, for both the children's sakes.

There would be plenty of time. Again she wondered why Kieran's stellar career as an emergency specialist had brought him to a small city way downunder in New Zealand. Could he have been thinking about Olivia when he'd applied? Was this his way of touching base with his niece without getting too involved? She doubted it. He hadn't exactly inundated the child with his attention since her parents had died. His communication over that time made a mute person seem verbose.

Abby tugged her blouse down over her hips and crossed to read the arrivals screen. Just where was this guy who had her little household all in a twitter? And who made her head spin with worry?

Kieran peered through the window down onto the glittering sea of horseshoe-shaped Tasman Bay. What a damned long way to come for two months' work. But he'd have gone to Siberia if that's what it took to please the chairman of the Board and further his own career. He sighed. He still didn't understand why the old boy thought it necessary for him to take a secondment overseas before he put in his application for head of the emergency department of Mercy Hospital in Dublin.

He'd been heading to Adelaide, Australia, for his secondment until this one in New Zealand had suddenly appeared. Adelaide had been the obvious choice. A much larger facility with higher patient numbers, which would look good on his CV. But Nelson required someone urgently as the current head of department had a very ill child needing care in Australia. Something about a liver transplant.

Even then Kieran had resisted, but whenever he'd glanced at the travel brochure on Nelson an image of a woman and one heated night of passion, the likes of which he'd never known before or since, had kept flicking across his mind.

Abigail. She lived in Nelson. Not that he intended picking up where they'd left off that night. No, thank you. That was a road to disaster. But the mental pictures of her and that one night had caused him to fill in the wrong set of papers.

Don't forget Olivia. It had broken his heart to watch her at the airport in Dublin, clinging to Abigail's hand as she had disappeared from his life through the bland doors of Immigration. Even knowing he'd done the best thing for Olivia hadn't made the pain any easier. He missed his sister, and Olivia was the only connection he had left to her. Two losses in one week had been horrendous. But no way would he change the arrangement. Olivia was far better off living with Abigail.

Kieran's hands clenched against his thighs as the plane shook and bucked. Why couldn't the pilot fly it in a straight line? Sweat slithered down between his shoulder blades, plastering his shirt to his skin.

A gnarled hand tapped his forearm. 'It's a bit bumpy, isn't it, dear?'

Kieran flicked a glance sideways at the elderly lady sitting beside him, her crotchet momentarily still in her lap. She didn't seem at all fazed by the turbulence. A benevolent smile and sparkling, washed-out blue eyes focused on him.

'Just a little,' he concurred, dragging out a smile.

'We won't be long now.'

'I certainly hope not.' He peered out the window looking for a distraction. But his mind quickly turned back to Abigail.

Of course, if he'd known of the bombshell she had been about to drop on him he'd definitely have chosen Adelaide. His muscles tensed. Would he? Truly? He shrugged, trying to ignore the multitude of questions that had buzzed around his skull since that phone call from her. Now here he was, minutes away from landing in her town. He shivered. Nelson. Where a whole bundle of difficult issues and decisions awaited him. And none of them medical.

A son. Abigail said the lad looked like him. Some alien emotion stirred within his chest, a feeling he didn't recognise. Surely not curiosity? Or pride?

Was it the familiar fear that he'd let Olivia down? And now Seamus? But how did a man who'd never experienced love from his parents love his own child? As his father had said often enough, he'd make a terrible parent. He didn't have it in him to love and care for children. The sooner he explained so that Abigail understood, the sooner her expectations about his role in the children's lives would disappear. For ever.

Just grand. He'd been coming for work, and now that had been pushed to the back of his mind with thoughts of Abigail and the children, making him feel rattled. Inadequate, even.

At least he'd be busy putting in long hours covering for staff on leave over Christmas and New Year. Apparently this was the time of year that Kiwis took their major holidays, spending weeks at the beaches, out in the mountains or following major sports events. At least there'd be time to get used to the idea of being a father and to decide how to deal with it.

'Don't bother. You'll make a mess of parenting, like you make a mess of most things in your life.' His father's voice slammed into his brain. The words that had spurred him to become an exceptional emergency specialist.

Bitterness soured his mouth as the old litany made its umpteenth rerun in his skull. He wasn't good at looking out for people he cared about. He'd known that since the day when Morag, his sister, had tripped and broken her ankle during a student party in his flat. She'd wrecked her chances at the European ski championships. In a blind fury their father had unfairly laid the blame firmly at Kieran's feet, telling him he was incapable of thinking of anyone except himself.

A fact his father had taken great delight in rubbing in again when Kieran's girlfriend at the time had miscarried. Kieran had been working late and hadn't had his cellphone switched on. His girlfriend had accused him of not being there when she'd needed him most. His father had added his taunt, saying that surely Kieran had finally learned his lesson and accepted he shouldn't get involved with anyone who would depend on him to look out for them.

Oh, he'd learned his lesson all right. He'd made a lifetime commitment to it. And nothing one little boy could do would change his mind.

Swallowing the bile rising in his throat, Kieran tried to focus on something brighter, less distressing. Abigail. Again. Funny how she popped straight into his mind. It had never once occurred to him that she'd be working in the same department he was going to. What if she insisted on being overly friendly at work? Worse, what if everyone already knew he was the father of her child? He cringed. That would put him on the back foot straight away. He was the head of the department, albeit temporarily, and fraternising with the staff was not good for staff relations.

Too late, boyo. The fraternising has been done, can't be undone. Abigail has a child, your child. A boy named Seamus.

He would do his damnedest to keep that information under wraps. If he wasn't already too late.

'I'd better not be,' he muttered.

All his muscles tightened. As they had done a thousand times on this trip whenever he thought about the situation. He still couldn't believe he was a father.

Was that because he didn't want to believe it?

He'd always taken care to avoid an accident of this kind. That's why he bought condoms by the ton. But he knew the boy was his. He knew Abigail wasn't one of those women who went from one man's bed to the next without a care. Neither would she use something like pregnancy to snag a man into marriage. If that had been her intention, she wouldn't have kept Seamus's arrival a secret from him. No, Abigail was honesty personified.

Discomfort made him squirm as he remembered that night in Dublin two years ago. Both of them had been totally smothered in grief after the joint funeral of his sister and Abigail's brother. They'd turned to each other for comfort, and for a few hours had forgotten everything as they'd discovered each other. He knew her all right. Intimately.

The plane shuddered. So did Kieran. His tense fingers ached, bent like claws. He squeezed his eyes tight. God, he hated flying. Think of something else, anything else. Abigail again. Wrong focus. But her image burned his eyeballs. As it had at unexpected moments ever since they'd made love.

'Did I hear an Irish accent?' Beside him the metal hook flicked in and out of the cotton. 'What brings you out here?'

A hurricane of waist-length dark blonde hair, and long arms and legs. A quirky smile that challenged him, and piercing hazel eyes that devoured him. Abigail.

No. He hadn't endured this agony to see her. 'I'm working at the local hospital. I also have a three-year-old niece living here.' *And your son. What about him?* If he mentioned Seamus then he was acknowledging the boy was a part of him. *I'm not ready for that.*

'They're a bundle of fun and tricks at that age. My grandson is into gardening at the moment, much to his mother's consternation, digging being his favourite occupation.'

'I can see how that could be a problem.' What did Olivia enjoy doing? Damn it, who does Olivia look like? His sister? Or David? How tall was she? He didn't know anything about her.

Appalled, he leaned his head back and stared at the moulded-plastic ceiling. He'd barely acknowledged any correspondence from Abigail about Olivia. He had behaved dreadfully, deliberately keeping out of touch. Arranging a regular money transfer from Dublin for Abigail to use for Olivia had been easy, and had salved his conscience whenever he'd thought there might be something he should be doing for his niece. No wonder Abigail hadn't contacted him about Seamus. She must have a very low opinion of him. Would she be waiting at the airport with a bat to bludgeon him over the head so she could drag him home to see the children? He forced his fingers straight, loose. Expanded his lungs. He couldn't blame her if she did.

Beside him the lady asked, 'So, your niece, is she a Kiwi?'

'Yes, she is, but she's Irish as well. My sister married a doctor from here, a friend of mine.' Best friend he'd ever had. 'They were killed in a car accident in Dublin a couple of years ago.'

'I'm very sorry to hear that.' The woman glanced at him. 'So the little girl has come over here to live with her father's family?'

'It seemed the best place for her, surrounded with lots of aunts and her grandfather. There's only me available on her mother's side and I live in the middle of Dublin. Not at all suitable for a small child.' *Not at all suitable for him.* Thankfully, David and Morag had it written into their wills that if anything should ever happen to them, he and Abigail would be Olivia's guardians, and she'd live with Abigail unless there was a very good reason why not. Which, of course, there wasn't. Abigail was very caring; perfect for a small, bewildered child who'd just lost her parents.

His companion nodded at the window. 'There's Nelson City. We'll be on the ground in a minute or two so you can relax now.'

'You aren't by any chance a psychologist?' he asked her.

'Just a canny old lady.'

'What are you doing in early February? I could do with you distracting me again when I head home.'

'I'm sure you could find a young lady to do that.'

That was absolutely the last thing he wanted. Or needed. He had a very comfortable lifestyle back in Dublin, one that didn't allow for anyone else interfering with his comings and goings. He'd created a perfect life that didn't involve...

anyone. Especially not a family. Not with his appalling credentials. Not even Olivia and Seamus could change his belief on that.

Seamus, a good Irish name. A clever move on Abigail's part? Or a name she liked more than any other? What did it matter what she'd called the lad? His jaw tightened some more. It shouldn't, but the fact that she'd had his child and not mentioned it right up until he was days from leaving Dublin galled. Which wasn't being fair to her. He knew he had a lot to make up to her for. But did he want to? It would mean getting to know the children, getting close to them. He shivered at the thought.

The plane's wheels thumped onto the tarmac. On the ground again. The end of his journey at last. Something unfurled in the pit of his stomach. The knot caused by his fear of flying? No, this felt different. Like…excitement. *No way.* Did he even know what it felt like to be really excited? Abigail's face floated into his mind, and the truth exploded through him. These feelings were all about her. The woman he'd never quite vanquished from his mind, from his body.

Suddenly he couldn't wait to see her, hug her, laugh with her.

Reason enough to stay aboard the plane and fly back the way he'd come.

CHAPTER TWO

ABBY's gaze was pulled to the plate-glass windows looking out over the tarmac and the disembarked passengers walking towards the terminal. Her nails dug painfully into her palms. One man towered above the rest of the passengers. Raven hair shining in the sun. A winning smile on a handsome face. He'd be exhausted after his long flight, but she'd never have guessed it from the way he carried himself. Shoulders back, legs swinging with confidence. As he came through the security door his gaze swept the terminal, searching. Then those twinkling eyes met hers and she saw the wariness in them. But then his smile broadened, oozing charm.

Her heart fluttered in her throat. That exact lopsided smile had once drawn her into bed with him. The urge to weep rose as unbidden memories teased at the fringes of her mind. Sweet memories of Kieran's face next to hers on a white pillow, of her fingers pushing through his dark curls as they'd lain entwined in the hotel's large bed, of his deep chuckle when she'd amused him.

It had been an unnatural time when emotions were raw, feelings bouncing all over the place. She'd be a fool to believe there was anything in those memories that could be rekindled now. She'd be a bigger fool to want anything close to that.

Remember, he's probably angry with you. As if she needed reminding. The ache in her stomach was testament to days of waiting and worrying about that. *This isn't some happy reunion of two friends. Kieran Flynn has come here to work. Not to see you. And to say they'd been friends would be stretching the facts a little.*

She gulped, tugged her shoulders back. Two children's happiness depended on her getting along with this man, who was now approaching her. But how to get around the fact that just seeing Kieran made her forget everything except him?

She studied Kieran. Sexy. The word banged into her head. Instantly she was back in that hotel bed with him. Her cheeks warmed. Her silly heart tripped. It wouldn't be easy, remaining neutral around Kieran. But she had to try. Starting right now.

'Hi, Kieran, welcome to Nelson.' Scintillating stuff, but her thought processes were mush. *Try to squash the longing. Hang on to the fact that you've deceived him.*

'Hello, Abigail.' And he dropped a light kiss on each cheek. Almost air kisses, kisses that meant absolutely nothing. Told her nothing. 'It's great to see you again.'

Oka-ay. The friendly approach. The friendly *playboy* approach. But, then, Kieran was known for his charm, so of course this would be second nature to him. She had to be careful not to be taken in by it all. She tried for a similar tone. 'Same. Good to see you, I mean.' Still making captivating conversation.

He stood, his arms hanging loosely at his sides. Aha. His fingers were tense. He wore a wary smile on his face. Waiting for something? A more welcoming response from her? What was she supposed to say to him? How was she supposed to greet him? She didn't know what he felt about the Seamus issue now that he'd had time to think about it. She hadn't a clue how he felt about her since her revelation.

His back was ramrod straight, his chin jutting out defensively. He lifted a hand towards her, let it drop. 'Thanks for coming to pick me up.'

Right, that helped. She knew exactly where she stood now. Not. Her hands fisted around her handbag strap. Then she got a whiff of that special Kieran scent of maleness and aftershave. She took a step back. A big step. That scent could undo all her resolve to remain neutral. It had lingered in the edges of her mind for two long, lonely years; teasing, annoying.

She forced a smile, worried he'd sense her unease. She hadn't forgotten how perceptive he could be. 'Kieran, I'm…' She sucked a breath, tried again. 'I'm really happy you've come. The family's looking forward to seeing you again.'

'How are they all? I guess the twins are out breaking the men's hearts these days.' This time he flashed a tired smile that had her feeling sympathetic towards him. Sympathy would draw her under his spell. That she couldn't afford. So ignore it.

'There have been a few casualties.' She straightened her back again, tried for a smile.

'Charlie and Steph have some parties lined up that you might like to go to.' Where there'd be plenty of single women for him to enjoy the company of. Abby felt a spurt of envy. She'd love to go to a party. With Kieran.

His black eyebrows rose. 'That's kind, but I'm going to have to disappoint them. I'm here to work, not socialise.'

'No one at the hospital expects you to spend the whole eight weeks tied to the A and E department. Dad's hoping you'll join the family for a meal on Friday night, and Olivia's so excited about you coming. And so is Seamus, although he doesn't really understand yet.' From few words to too many. Brain mush again.

He stepped back, looked around cautiously. 'They're not here? With you?' His glance settled on a little girl standing with a small group of people next to them.

Oh, my goodness, he doesn't know what Olivia looks like. 'They're at home with their nanny.'

As he turned back and gave her another cautious smile, she added, 'I've been working today. I was given time off to meet you, and take you to your apartment.'

'Thank you, I really appreciate it.' His smile

tugged at her heart, made her momentarily forget why she'd been so nervous.

She found her mouth lifting in a return smile. 'You didn't give me much choice.'

'Bit abrupt, was I?' His blue eyes fixed her to the floor.

'Just a weensy bit.' She nodded, biting down on the smile. She looked up into his face, and again felt her stomach muscles tighten with apprehension. How would she survive having Kieran living in her home town? Working in the ED department as her boss? Visiting his niece and son in her cottage? If he visited them. Of course he'd visit them. He had to.

Right now she was stunned at the depth of feeling she had for this enigmatic man tripping her up at every turn. She hadn't expected that. Get back on track, the common-sense side of her brain warned. This was the day of reckoning, the day when she'd learn how Kieran intended dealing with the fact he was a father. It had been a long time coming, and yet she had always known it would come. Even if she'd had to wait another year, another five years, it would have come.

And she would never have been ready.

* * *

'You've cut your hair,' Kieran commented, feeling a pang of loss.

'Too hard to manage with small children and their sticky fingers.' She flashed him a half-smile.

She had beautiful hair. Even now. Cut in a soft style that tucked around her face Kieran wanted to reach out and touch the silky strands. He resisted with difficulty. Touching her would not help the situation.

Abigail's nervous with me. She was trying to hide it but her give-away facial expressions told the truth. Pique rippled through him. He wasn't used to being treated in such a deliberately off-hand fashion. Of course she'd be apprehensive after shocking him about Seamus, but he'd just spent nearly two days travelling around the globe so he didn't appreciate being treated like something dragged up from the bottom of a deep pond. He was the one who had something to be upset about. And hadn't he been charming and friendly?

'I apologise for the brevity of my email, but there seemed to be hundreds of things to be organised before I left home.' He risked another smile. His smiles usually won him anything he wanted.

Abigail leaned closer, a whiff of some exotic flower tantalising him. She was no doubt only now recognising that she hadn't been very welcoming. How would she make up for that? A light kiss?

She said, 'Baggage claim's outside.'

Great. Getting warmer. His heart banged against his ribs. He'd have to polish his charm if the next two months were to be bearable. 'Right, let's grab my gear and get out of here.'

As he turned to follow her, the old lady who had sat next to him on the plane waved and called softly, 'You won't be needing me next trip.' Her head tilted at Abigail.

Oh, yes, he would. He might want to win a warm smile from the woman who'd shanghaied his brain but he couldn't imagine taking a long-haul flight with her and Olivia. And Seamus, a little voice piped up in the back of his head. He winked at the old lady. 'See you in February.'

Then he strode outside to the baggage claim area. As he did so he thought about the unexpected change in the warm, vibrant woman standing next to him. He'd first met her at his sister's marriage to David. Abigail seemed quieter, more uptight than he recalled. Guess being a mother did that.

He totted up other changes he'd begun noticing. Abigail didn't bounce on her toes any more. Her quick grin seemed to have flicked off permanently. Shadows lined the skin beneath her eyes. Life since they'd spent that wonderful night together had been harder on her than him.

A screech of tyres snapped through the air, followed by a thump. A woman screamed.

Another woman cried out, 'Quick. Someone, help.'

Kieran met Abigail's startled glance. 'That our cue?'

She nodded, 'I'd say so.'

'I'm a doctor.' Kieran squeezed past gaping faces and prodding elbows.

Abigail followed. 'Let me through. I'm a nurse.'

'He stepped right in front of me.' A male voice sounded defensive. 'I never had a chance to avoid him.'

Abigail dropped to her knees beside a prostrate man held down at his chest by the front wheel of a four-wheeled motorbike towing the baggage trailers.

Looking around, Kieran said, 'Someone, call an ambulance.'

'I'm onto it,' a man answered.

Urgency underlined Abigail's words. 'We need that bike lifted away.'

Kieran searched the closest faces, found the driver of the bike, an orange safety jacket and a white face the give-away. 'How many of us will it take to move this bike?'

'Six, I reckon. I'll unhook the luggage trailers.' The man's voice trembled as he stared down at the accident victim. 'Is he going to be all right?'

Kieran gripped the driver's shoulder. 'We can't say until we've had a proper look at him.'

'He kind of tripped. I never saw him coming.'

Tripped? Stepped out? Fainted? Heart attack? Kieran tossed up scenarios. The unconscious man appeared to be in his late forties, maybe early fifties, so cardiac malfunction couldn't be ruled out.

Turning to the pressing crowd, he spoke loudly and clearly. 'Step back, everyone. Give us some space, please.' He searched for strong men to help lift the quad bike away.

'Abigail, you'll have to move aside for a moment.' He didn't want her getting hurt if the lift went wrong and the bike toppled over.

She nodded. When their patient had been freed, she leaned close to him. 'You weren't meant to start work today.'

'If you mean, am I alert enough after thirty-six hours' flying? No, I'm probably not up to a full-scale emergency. But I think we can manage this between us.' At least the patient might be happier to have him around than she appeared to be.

A shadow crossed her eyes, darkening them to the colour of well-cooked toast. 'I only meant it's not much of a welcome to Nelson.'

He squeezed her hand, suddenly in need of contact with her. Any contact. He wanted to establish a connection that would get him over the hurdles of the coming weeks. 'Let's look at our man.'

They knelt, one each side of their patient, and Abigail lifted the man's wrist as he opened his eyes slowly, blinking in the bright daylight.

'What happened?' he croaked.

'You've been knocked down by a quad bike,' Kieran explained. 'I'm Dr Flynn, and this is

Abby Brown, a nurse. Can you tell me your name and address, please?'

As he answered, Abigail counted his pulse rate.

'Paul Stokes, three Caper Drive, Richmond.'

Nothing wrong with the man's coherence. Kieran gently felt Paul's chest. 'I'm checking your ribs for fractures.'

He didn't add that if any ribs had been staved in a lung might be punctured. Pneumothorax was a distinct, and very serious, possibility.

His patient grunted through white lips, beads of perspiration covered his forehead. 'It hurts like hell. When I breathe in.'

Around them people jostled for a look at the unfortunate man while others quickly collected their bags and disappeared.

Abby placed Paul's wrist down at his side. 'Pulse is elevated. The paramedics can run an ECG when they arrive.'

Kieran nodded, and asked their patient, 'Do you remember feeling any chest pain before you were knocked down?'

Paul's voice was weakening. 'I felt odd. Like I couldn't quite get enough air into my lungs.'

The words dragged out around his pain, his red face now grey.

'Did you notice the bike before it ran into you?' Kieran was aware of Abigail carefully checking their patient's legs for any injuries inflicted when the bike had rammed him.

'No. Just my weird breathing.'

Abigail muttered, 'There's swelling along the thigh, but no blood seepage. I'd like to remove these jeans and have a closer look at his right leg.'

'It'll have to wait,' Kieran replied. 'Okay, Paul, try to relax.' He asked Abigail quietly, 'Just how far away is the nearest hospital?'

A slow smile curved her lips and burned him with its warmth. At last, the Abigail he'd been looking for. 'Nearest hospital? The only hospital. You're not in Dublin now.' Her smile widened, taking away any sting he might've found in her words. 'The ambulance base is ten minutes from here if they get a clear run.'

Paul groaned, flapped his hands over his chest. 'Worse,' he gasped. His eyes closed, and his head rolled to the side.

Immediately Abigail located his neck pulse, shook her head. 'Nothing.'

Cardiac arrest. Just what they needed. Kieran fisted his hand and gave a hard thump to Paul's chest but the heart didn't restart. 'Compressions. Quick, or we'll lose him.'

Abigail tilted the man's head back to open his airway while Kieran placed his interlocked hands over Paul's heart. As he pressed down and began counting the compressions, his admiration for Abigail's efficiency crept through his mind. From the moment they'd first heard the dreadful thud of Paul taking a slam she'd been one step ahead of him. Now she held the man's head, no doubt ready to take over the compressions if required.

Kieran continued the compressions. 'Thirty.' At his nod Abby checked Paul's carotid pulse, shook her head. Kieran pressed down again. Thirty compressions. No pulse. Somewhere beyond the terminal a siren screamed. *Please let it be the ambulance.*

Abby placed her forefinger on the carotid artery. 'Come on, Paul, breathe for us.'

Kieran pressed down, heard Abby gasp, 'I think we have a pulse. Her mouth curved into a tender smile as she nodded. 'Yes, definitely.'

Kieran sagged in relief. 'Thank goodness

for that.' He glanced up as the paramedics arrived. They would take over now. He grinned at Abigail. 'We make a great team.'

Her smile wavered. 'We do.' She placed a hand on his arm and leaned close. Then suddenly jerked backwards.

Had she been about to kiss him? Disappointment surged through his tired body. If only she had. He squashed the urge to haul her into his arms and kiss her. Properly. He had not come here to rekindle their fling. That had been a one-night, grief-blanking event. It had been absolutely magical, but never to be repeated. Sadness swamped him. Never? *Never.*

A sigh rippled across his bottom lip. 'At least we know we work well together.'

'We know more than that.' Then she slam-dunked him. 'We also made a beautiful little boy together.'

'So that's our new boss.' Sally stood behind the nurses' station in the emergency department, ogling Kieran as he chatted to two nurses. Two female nurses, who were having trouble keeping their jaws off the floor.

'Yep, that's him.' Abby sighed wistfully. He

already looked as though he belonged there. Five minutes and he had the staff eating out of his hand.

Kieran had come in from the airport in the ambulance with Paul Stokes. It hadn't been necessary but he'd insisted, saying he'd feel happier about the situation. The female paramedics had acquiesced to his charm within seconds. Abby had screwed up the parking ticket she'd found under her windscreen wiper and followed the ambulance, her car filled with Kieran's luggage. If she hadn't known better she'd have thought he'd come for a year. But she did know better. Even if he finally accepted his son, Kieran wouldn't be staying. His career always came first. Why was that? Did he continuously have to prove himself, like someone else she'd known?

'Very tasty.' Sally almost drooled.

'You think so?' Abby glanced in the same direction as her friend and felt a hitch in her throat as Kieran bent over the cardiac monitoring equipment attached to his patient, stretching his trousers across a very tidy backside. But totally agreeing with her closest friend didn't mean she had to admit it out loud.

Happily married, Sally was in the business of finding Abby a husband, so far without success. Mainly because Abby had no interest in settling down with anyone ever again. She'd tried it once and had been scorched so badly she no longer trusted her own judgment.

'Whenever you speak in that so-who-gives-a-damn voice I know you're covering your real thoughts. Come on, what harm can it do to admit the guy's gorgeous?' A smug look settled over Sally's face. 'He's single, right?'

'Don't go there. I am not the slightest bit tempted. Believe me on this one.' Abby huffed out a breath and turned away from the intriguing sight. She had to stop Sally in her tracks. It didn't help that her friend didn't know who Seamus's father was. Abby had never divulged that information, and Sally had quickly learned not to mention it. 'I am definitely not interested.'

'Not interested in what?' asked the man himself from behind her.

Sheesh. Her hands fisted in her tunic pockets. She'd been so intent on getting the message through Sally's skull that she hadn't noticed Kieran leave his patient and cross over to them.

'Nothing,' she muttered.

'Are you sure?' Kieran's gaze scudded over her.

'Absolutely.' A shiver tickled her spine but she met his gaze head on, and gulped. His eyes, so bright, so perceptive, held her enthralled. She'd been expecting anger, not beguiling smiles and twinkling eyes. With an extreme effort she looked away, fully aware that Kieran was quite capable of seducing her into a false sense of ease before he delivered his attack about Seamus. She held no illusions that a diatribe would come. Why not? She'd behaved badly over this.

'Hello, Abby?' Kieran waved his hand before her. 'Where have you gone?'

She shook her head. Not very far at all. She seemed to have lost her grip on reality today. 'How's Paul Stokes?' She nodded in their patient's direction in the hope of deflecting Kieran. 'How's the latest ECG looking?'

Kieran continued to study her in that disturbing manner that made her want to check whether she had any clothes on. Finally, he replied to her query. 'Not good. Who's the duty cardiologist? How do I get hold of him?'

Sally took over. 'Hamish Harrington, and I'll track him down for you.'

'Has the patient's wife been called?'

When Sally nodded, Kieran turned back to Abby. 'Can you give me a quick tour of the department and introduce me to the staff? Paul's in good hands with the intern until the cardiologist gets here.'

With his hand firmly holding her elbow, she had little choice except to do as he'd asked. But as the nurse in charge of the department Sally should be the one to show him around. 'Sally? You want to do this?'

One wink from Sally and Abby knew there'd be no help from that quarter. Her friend would actively foster any interest that Kieran might show in her.

Tugging her arm free, Abby answered, 'It won't take long. It's not a huge department such as you'll be used to.'

'Makes an interesting change. There might be more time to get to know the staff than I have back home.'

Abby rolled her eyes. 'Unfortunately, we still get incredibly busy. As with any hospital board, finance rules. Staffing levels are usually at least one, if not two, people below what we require.'

'Typical.' Kieran shrugged. 'Dr Banning mentioned that this hospital services a huge rural area.'

It was Michael Banning's position as Head of Department that Kieran would be covering.

Abby filled Kieran in. 'The whole of the top of the South Island really, apart from Blenheim, which is more than a hundred kilometres away. There are small rural towns and plenty of farms, orchards and vineyards fanning out from here, plus major industries such as forestry and fishing.'

'Both those industries are susceptible to hideous accidents.'

'You're not wrong there.' Abby's lips pressed together and a flicker of despair cramped her stomach. Twice she'd nursed old school friends after logging accidents.

Kieran was right behind her when she pushed open the door to Michael's, soon to be Kieran's, office, the last stop on the tour. She felt so aware of him that her skin seemed to have a life of its own; a hot tingle touching the insides of her elbows, a searing on her neck just below her chin. She took a large step inside to put space between them, and turned to face Kieran.

The door clicked shut, and Kieran leaned back against it, his unfathomable eyes fixed on her. A shiver of trepidation chilled her. Was this it? Had the moment she'd been dreading arrived? Here? At work? Surely not.

She swallowed around the lump in her throat. 'It's a pity Michael couldn't be here to meet you but, of course, he's incredibly tied up at the moment and not expecting you to come in until Friday.'

'Abigail.' He stopped, shook his head. 'You're not comfortable with me being here, in the department, are you?' His bewilderment appeared genuine. His chin lifted and those blue eyes darkened as he waited for her reply.

'It's a little awkward, with what's between us. I— You…' She stopped. *Even today, every time he looks at me, I want to put my hands on his face, run my fingers along that strong jaw. I want one of his bone-bending kisses. No, I don't. I want to run away from the questions in those tired eyes.* 'We do need to talk about Seamus, but I don't think this is the place. Right now you have a patient to hand over and then you should get out of here while you can. You're exhausted from your trip, and in need of a meal and a shower.'

For a long moment Kieran stared at her. Abby shoved her trembling fingers deep into her pockets as she waited for him to tell her what he really thought about her decision not tell him about his son.

Finally, Kieran jerked the handle to open the door. But his voice was surprisingly soft, almost sympathetic. 'We've not finished talking, but you're right, it'll have to wait until a more suitable time and place.'

'Thank goodness.' Relief whooshed through Abby.

Kieran raised a black eyebrow. 'There's nothing to be thankful for. We have one hell of a mess to sort out.'

'Mess?' That was not how she'd describe her family but, then, she wasn't the one terrified of raising children. 'Listen, Kieran. I love those kids and believe I'm giving them everything they need to grow into happy, responsible adults. Where's the mess in that?'

'I only have one…' He hesitated. 'Sorry, two relatives, and they both live on the opposite side of the world from me. I never know what is happening in their lives. Until a few days ago, I didn't even know there was a second child I should be aware of. This, to me, is a mess.'

He had a valid point. Despite the photos and Olivia's drawings she'd sent him, he didn't really know his niece. Whose fault was that? But they weren't really talking about Olivia. It was Seamus who hung between them, divided them.

'You wouldn't believe the number of times I tried to ring and tell you about Seamus. I even wrote letters to you, included photos in with some of them.'

'Odd I never got them.' Disbelief dripped off his tongue in great dollops.

Hurt, she cried out, 'I can give them to you any time you want. I've still got them all.'

'I don't see the point now.' He turned toward the door, the conversation over. At least the disbelief had abated. Then he looked over his shoulder at her. 'One thing. Do any of the staff here know I'm the father of your son?'

'Absolutely not.'

'There's something I can be grateful for, then.'

Raw pain gripped her. Was he ashamed of his

son? In all the scenarios her mind had tossed up, not one had included Kieran feeling like that. Shame she could not cope with. 'You're not giving any of us a chance.'

His smile was professional; confident and cool. 'You think so? How's this for a chance? I'll visit you and the children later this afternoon. Will that suit you?'

And if it didn't? But she could see in his now chilly eyes that he wouldn't take no for an answer. Anyway, she wanted him to see the kids, meet his son. She wanted it over and done with. Her stomach couldn't take too much more tension. 'Come for dinner. Six o'clock.' Obviously he didn't want her to deliver him to his apartment.

'You eat dinner at six?'

'No, the children do. We'll eat after they go to bed.'

He pulled the door open, held it wide for her to pass through. 'You still live on the same road as when I was here for the wedding?'

She sighed. What did he know about any of them? 'Yes, but don't forget I'm in the cottage next to the orchard. David and Morag's place.'

'I'll see you at six, then.' He strode along

to the nurses' station, leaving her shaking in his wake.

She stared at his ramrod back and wished him back in Ireland. Then she'd be able to go back to the simple problems of raising two small children while holding down a responsible job, of making her dollars go twice as far as they were intended to, of looking out for her father and high-maintenance twin sisters. Easy, compared to dealing with an angry, hurt man who had claim to her family.

CHAPTER THREE

KIERAN'S head pounded, and his eyes were gritty. He drove carefully, aware of the tiredness threatening to engulf him. That enormous bed back in the apartment arranged for his stay had been tempting but, given the state of his mind, sleep would've been impossible.

Why the hell had he said he'd go out to the cottage tonight? What had happened to the idea of getting settled before seeing the children? Abigail had happened, that's what. Damn, but she got to him so easily. So much for his re-nowned self-control.

HOPE. The green road sign drew his attention, and he eased his foot off the accelerator. If he remembered correctly, the turn-off to Abigail's place wasn't much further.

HOPE. The small community that boasted one store and a café, a cluster of houses, and or-chards for as far as he could see. He swallowed as goose-bumps lifted his skin. A community. A place where families grew up. Families like Max Brown's. Max was Abigail's father and had raised four children in this district, had buried his wife here, lost his son in a tragic accident, welcomed his granddaughter. And his grandson. Don't forget Seamus, his brain nagged.

His son. As if he could forget the boy. Even when he tried to, the unsettling situation remained firmly fixed in his mind.

Kieran pulled off the road in front of the sign, the engine of his hired car idling. His hands were slick with sweat, and he rubbed them down his jeans. In a few minutes he'd meet his son for the first time. His gut clenched, his breathing became shallow. It wasn't too late to turn back to the apartment.

To be sure, Abigail would understand. Who was he fooling? A family girl through and through, she might think she understood his struggle with coming face to face with Seamus for the first time, but she'd be wide of the mark. Abby didn't know he had nothing to offer apart from money. For him to give unconditional love to a small child was the same as someone trying to breathe without lungs. Impossible.

No way would Abigail comprehend how different his life had been from hers. She had roots here, while, with his father in the diplomatic service, the world had been Kieran's community. Boarding schools and sterile apartments in countless cities hadn't given him a sense of belonging anywhere.

What had it been like for Abigail, growing up here? When she'd left home she'd crossed the orchard and moved into the cottage that used to belong to her brother and his wife and which was now held in trust for Olivia. A narrow life? Or a free, all-encompassing way to live? At least she knew where she belonged. She had somewhere to return to, people to turn to, whenever life went belly up.

Abigail. Twice at the airport while they had been administering to Stokes he'd called her Abby. He didn't know why but until then he'd always used her full name. Except that night when they'd made love. Then Abigail had seemed wrong for the passionate woman in his arms, stroking his body, revitalising his jaded outlook on life, and making him briefly question his lifestyle.

Kieran nodded at the sign. HOPE. Could that

be the peculiar sensation tapping under his ribs? Did this place hold the answers to all those emotions he was afraid to face? Warmth trickled through him. Odd, when he should've been feeling a chill at the thought.

Checking the road was clear, he pulled out and headed towards Abigail's house. To his future? Or to trouble? Only time would tell. All he could be sure of was that he was about to meet his son.

As he turned into Abigail's road his stomach did such violent flips he thought he would be sick. A thin line of sweat rolled down past his jaw. His teeth clenched, aching.

Get a grip. He could not be seen to be failing at this first encounter. Damn it, he was thirty-five years old, a doctor, a man who'd stood up to drunken thugs on a Friday night in the emergency department. He would not be bested by a fifteen-month-old toddler.

Says who?

'Welcome to Rose Cottage.' Abigail opened the narrow gate at the end of a footpath leading to a small weatherboard house.

'Thank you. Were you waiting out here for me?' Kieran reached for the gate, his hand inadvertently brushing against hers. The brief touch sent a zing up his arm and into his already fried brain. One innocent little touch and he dropped further out of his depth.

'Not quite. Olivia's so excited about you coming and I caught her on the roadside, trying to look for you. I figured a game on the lawn might distract her.' Abby pointed to a little girl charging along the path in their direction. 'Here she comes now.'

Kieran let the gate slam behind him. Then promptly leaned against it for strength. Pain stabbed his chest as he watched this bundle of arms and legs and dark curls hurtling towards him. His sister as a child. Memories swamped him. Frightened him. It had been his fault Morag had had an accident and ruined her career. And this little girl was the spitting image of his sister. Was he a danger to her, too?

Shaking his head to dispel the stranglehold these thoughts had on him, he tried to move. Couldn't. Paralysed by memories evoked by a three-year-old. Him! Dr Flynn. Dr Cool, Calm and Collected. Mr Charming with the ladies. What could he possibly say to Olivia?

Olivia didn't suffer the same problem. 'Uncle Kieran, Uncle Kieran, here I am.'

Uncle. His mouth fell open. Uncle. He swallowed around the ache in his throat. He was an uncle. Here was the living proof.

Thump. She slammed into his knees, her arms reaching for him. Was he supposed to pick her up? Hug her? Hesitantly he leaned down and lifted her up to hold her warm body against his trembling frame, his arm muscles tense. She was warm and soft and unable to stay still. Her fingers touched his face and he jerked his head back, stunned at the unexpected contact. Slowly he let his head fall forward again. Thankfully Olivia was turning around in his arms, grabbing at his hands, still making him feel totally lost.

Abigail watched them in that enigmatic way of hers. Did she find him lacking? She'd have to give him time to become familiar with his role in Olivia's life. Would two months be enough to learn the art of being an uncle? A good uncle? Not to mention being a father. How did one go about being a father? He had no idea. And had no intention of learning.

Where was Seamus? Looking around, he couldn't see a toddler anywhere. He felt weird, disorientated, expecting to see his son. And now, with Olivia in his arms, everything as he knew it was unravelling. What used to be real for him had become a murky picture in his head. In the short space of time it had taken to get from his car to holding Olivia, his comfortable life seemed to be changing. That was plain scary. His mouth dried. Terrifying, really. He did not want his life to change. He loved it exactly as it had been until this moment.

Focus on Olivia. She, he might be able to handle. If he had a fairy godmother hovering overhead. 'Olivia's full of energy,' he said lamely.

'Amazing what the promise of a visit from Uncle Kieran does.' Abby finally gave him a full-blown, power-packed smile that sent all thoughts of children miles from his mind. Sweet longing for that special connection they'd once known shot down to his toes. He'd missed her. The knowledge slammed through him, rocked him back on his heels. *He had missed her.* It couldn't be possible after such a short liaison. But he found no other explanation for the hollow feeling in his chest. He'd missed Abby, and now he was with her he felt the ground rolling under his feet. Was it too late to pull out of his contract and return to Dublin?

Sticky hands again touched his face. 'Do you like me, Uncle Kieran?'

Kieran gulped, refocused on his niece. 'Absolutely, Princess.' And to his surprise he found he meant it. 'Absolutely.'

'Abby, he likes me.'

'Of course. Who wouldn't?'

Abby slipped past them, her hip brushing against him, tightening the longing that threatened to unravel his precarious rein on his emotions. Had to be the jet-lag. Or the shock of seeing Olivia after all this time. Or the apprehension about coming face to face with his son. This odd sensation of drowning in need-filled sweetness couldn't have anything to do with Abby. Abigail. Stick to calling her Abigail and he might be able to banish thoughts of that night they'd shared.

He followed her, his lively bundle twisting and turning in his arms as they walked down a path overgrown with roses. As Abigail entered the house she turned back to him. 'Seamus is with Dad, having a ride on the tractor.'

Kieran swallowed a tug of disappointment.

Ha, gotcha. You were looking forward to seeing your son for the first time. He gulped, checked to see if Abigail had noticed.

She winked at him. 'Seamus will be driving before he can talk at this rate. Dad spends hours taking him for rides on either the four-wheel bike or tractor.'

'But he's only one. Surely it's not very safe for someone that young.' Worry flared. This was his son they were talking about.

Abigail looked at him as though she knew exactly what he was thinking, and a triumphant smile lifted her mouth. 'Dad drives so slowly snails pass them. He also straps Seamus into a harness fitted to him, otherwise I'd be the first to stop them.'

'I guess you would.' He didn't doubt she'd be a very responsible parent. His concern ebbed. He shouldn't be worrying, that was Abigail's job.

She twisted away on her feet. 'Come inside. Make yourself at home.' Then she smiled over her shoulder at the girl he held. 'Bath time, missy.'

'I don't want one,' Olivia answered from the safety of his arms.

'Now, why doesn't that surprise me?' Abigail

stood with one hand on her hip. 'The only time you like water is when it's in a muddy puddle.'

Kieran asked Olivia, 'Don't you want to be clean for me?'

'No.'

'Do you want Uncle Kieran to bath you?'

What? Did he get any say in this? He wouldn't know where to start when it came to bathing small children.

It was time he went back to town and the relative safety of his apartment. A haven from his niece and her expectations of him.

'I want Abby to bath me.'

Relief poured through his tense muscles as he put Olivia down. Warily he followed her through the house. What would it be like to share bathtimes with your kids? It might be fun.

Whoa. Back up. Bathing a child meant getting involved and he didn't do involvement. Funny how his resolve seemed to be slipping away so fast within hours of arriving. If he had already started wondering about bathtime, what would he be doing by the end of his two-month spell here? He had to remain focused on the purpose of his visit, which was to run ED, not to become enmeshed in this family.

'If you want a glass of wine or a beer, you'll find some at the back of the fridge, top shelf.' Abby swung Olivia up into her arms in a graceful movement that drew his eyes to her curves.

Abigail. Her name was Abigail. So what if today she walked and talked more like an Abby? Looking nothing like the slim, almost anorexic women he usually dated, her height and voluptuousness fascinated him. The night of passion they'd shared in Dublin still slammed into his head at the most unexpected moments. Often in the middle of the night when he couldn't sleep he'd think of the Kiwi woman who'd shared his grief in the most intimate way imaginable. Her brother, his sister. Both gone, all because of a teenager who'd thought driving his mother's car would be easy. Abigail's big, sad eyes had drawn him to her and, like an alcoholic to the bottle, he'd had to have her.

It hadn't been enough. It should've been. He didn't do commitment. Commitment meant love, and Abigail was the kind of woman that eventually would want, would deserve, commitment and love. He couldn't give any woman love. Abigail hadn't grown up learning the hard lessons about relationships that he had got from his father. Thankfully, Morag, being the apple of their father's eye, hadn't suffered the knocks he had, hadn't grown the hard shell around her heart that he had.

Stop the thinking. Grab a beer and relax. As the cool liquid rolled across his tongue he looked around. Abby had created a cosy atmosphere, perfect for young children. The bright blues and apricots on the walls and in the furnishings were warm and vibrant. Just like the woman herself. The furniture had seen better days so she obviously didn't use the money he sent on anything other than Olivia. If she used it at all. It occurred to him that she mightn't have touched a single cent.

But this was all about the children. What about Abigail? Surely she got lonely for adult company at night? He was assuming she spent the nights alone, but was probably wrong.

Piercing giggles coming from somewhere along the short hallway drew his attention. Before he could think about what he was doing he followed the sound. Stopping in the bathroom doorway, he leaned against the doorjamb and watched Abby bath Olivia. He had to swallow hard to get the next mouthful of beer past the lump in his throat. The bath was filled with soap bubbles, and Abby wore her share of them on her cheeks and forehead. She looked gorgeous.

He cleared his throat. 'If Olivia gets this much fun out of a bath then I can't begin to imagine her excitement in those puddles you mentioned.'

'It gets fairly messy.' Abby tugged a towel from the rail and lifted a protesting Olivia out of the water. 'Let's get you dry, little missy. Seamus will be here in a minute and he'll need scrubbing from top to toe.'

Kieran gulped and returned to the kitchen, feeling useless and out of his depth. The door looked very tempting. A few strides and he could be at his car. His son would be here any minute. His heart felt oddly out of whack as he grappled with the enormity of that. The moment he'd been dreading since Abigail's phone call was racing towards him. He wasn't ready. He'd never be ready. He stared around, panic beginning to boil up. He needed something to occupy his brain. A bag of groceries lay on the bench. Peering inside, he found steak and salad vegetables. Some of the tension tightening his shoulders eased. Cooking steak and tossing together a salad he could do blindfolded.

Just then the back door flew open. A deep voice he recognised as Max Brown's was telling someone, presumably Seamus, to slow down or he'd trip. A little boy tumbled into the kitchen, his clothes covered in grass stains. His chubby face was red and he was chattering nonstop in gibberish.

Kieran's hand stopped halfway out of the grocery bag. His breath stuck in his lungs. The time had come. No getting out of this one. What if he got it all wrong? Said or did the wrong thing? Scared the boy off so they'd never get along? He dropped the packet of steak back in the bag. He was out of here. Now. Before Seamus came any closer, before the boy caught his eye and turned him into a complete blithering idiot. Damn it, he should've left when he'd had the chance instead of dithering around procrastinating.

Then Abigail was standing beside him, her hand reaching for his, and it was too late. He couldn't leave now. The tremor in her fingers surprised him. When he lifted his eyes to hers he saw his own fear and trepidation mirrored there. Her teeth were digging hard into her bottom lip. Turning his hand over, he twined his fingers through hers. Knowing this might be as hard for her as it was for him made everything just a little bit easier.

He whispered through his blocked throat, 'Introduce me to our son.'

She blinked. 'Sure.' But she didn't move a muscle.

'Come on, Abby, we can do this.' Really?

Another blink. Then, inclining her head in acknowledgement, she turned to face the man and toddler waiting expectantly. 'Hey, Dad. Seamus…' She dropped to her knees and lifted the dark-haired boy against her, hugged him tight for a moment, as though afraid to let him go. Afraid to share him? No, not Abby. She wanted this. Didn't she?

As the boy squirmed to be set free, Abby stood up and held him so Kieran could take a good look at him. 'Seamus, love, this is Uncle Kieran.' She raised troubled eyes to Kieran. 'Sorry, I'm not sure what you want to be called, and Olivia has been talking about her uncle all week.'

Kieran stood spellbound. This was his son. His own flesh and blood. There was no denying the wide, full mouth came from the Flynn side. Seamus had the black hair and blue eyes that all Flynns seemed to inherit, but the expression in those eyes gawping at him was pure Abby. Kieran could've wept. He felt his heart dissolving. The boy was beautiful. His boy. Was this how every father felt when he saw his child for the very first time? Frightened? Protective? Lungs all gummed up so he couldn't breathe?

The silence in the tiny kitchen was deafening. Kieran couldn't have spoken a single word if his life had depended on it. All the arguments he'd had for not wanting a part in this boy's life evaporated faster than ice cream in a desert. He lifted his arms to take Seamus and was rewarded with a toothless grin. Somewhere under his ribs he felt a sharp stab. Of love? Whoa. He was not ready for this. If this was unconditional love then he wasn't ready, wasn't capable of doing it. It frightened him. Like bungee-jumping without a cord.

Then his arms were filled with a wriggling toddler. He grasped Seamus with stiff fingers, held him awkwardly out from his chest. And stared down at him. Seamus. A huge lump blocked his throat, cut off his breathing. He drank in the sight of his son, aware of every wriggle, every thump of one tiny fist on his arm. He saw big eyes peering up at him, trusting him. He saw innocence so sweet it made his knees weak. His heart felt as though it would explode right out through his ribs. This was what it felt like to be a parent. This simple. This terrifying.

He couldn't do it. He wasn't father material. What if he harmed Seamus with his ineptitude? Seamus needed love and caring and twenty-four-hour attention. Not a dried-up shell of a man for whom the closest thing to love was sharing a bed with a warm woman for a night.

He turned to hand the boy back to Abigail, to put him aside, back to where he'd be loved. But Abigail took a step away. What? She wasn't going to rescue her child? The panic he'd felt earlier threatened to erupt. He clenched his muscles and Seamus wriggled against him in protest. See? Already he had made a mistake. *Suck in a breath. Deeply. Let it out, ride the panic. Another deep breath. I can't do this.*

'Grandad, Grandad.' Olivia's shouts filled the cottage, and Max leaned over to shake his hand, saying above the din, 'Welcome to Nelson, lad. It's great to have you here.'

Kieran shook his head in an attempt to clear away the overwhelming emotions engulfing him. The panic calmed. 'Thanks, Max.' He huffed the air from his lungs. 'It's good to see you, too.' Loosening his grip on Seamus and trying to hold him with one arm, he managed to return the handshake. He hadn't been called 'lad' since boarding-school days, and never in the friendly tone Abby's father had used.

So did Max know he was Seamus's father? If so, what did the older man think of him? Maybe Max had called him 'lad' to soften him up before getting him into a corner and telling him exactly what he expected from Kieran for his grandson. And for his daughter.

Abigail was very quiet. Kieran looked around, found her regarding him steadily. Then she leaned close. 'Isn't he gorgeous?'

He stared down at Seamus, at the complete trust reflected in the young eyes looking back at him. Assessing *him*? Did Seamus see the fear? The emptiness? Gazing back, Kieran saw no sign of the crushing defeat of a child who strived, and failed, to be loved by his parent. With Abby for a mother it was unlikely he ever would. Thank goodness.

But the same couldn't be said about Seamus's father. The boy deserved better. Somewhere behind his ribs he felt something sharp, like he had a stitch from a long run. A painful stitch. Was he going to give away his chance with this child before he'd had time to get to know him? If he knew what was right for the boy he should. But…it wouldn't be easy to walk away now. It would've been better all round if he hadn't met the lad. Now he knew what Seamus looked like, knew how it felt to hold him.

'Kieran?' Abigail nudged him. 'Don't you think he's great?'

He could only manage, 'He's beautiful.' His eyes still focused on Seamus, his arms reluctant to let the boy go even when he knew he should. Before he became too involved.

Max told the room at large, 'I'll be off. I'm going out for dinner. Catch up with you at the weekend, Kieran, when you've had time to settle in.'

Kieran was vaguely aware of Max hugging his granddaughter before leaving. Then of Olivia turning on the TV, and Abby quietly telling her to turn the volume down. Kieran tugged out a chair from the kitchen table and dropped onto it, still holding his son, now very tenderly. *Almost as though afraid he'll break.*

As Seamus forced a thumb into his mouth

Abby sauntered in and leaned against the bench, relief lightening her face. 'He's taken to you, no problems.'

'How can you be so sure this soon?' Kieran heard the edge in his voice, and cursed silently. Abby had been as nervous about this meeting as he had, and now she seemed to be handling it all right. Why couldn't he?

'You'd know if Seamus didn't want to go near you. He has a set of lungs on him you wouldn't believe. Must have got them from your side.'

'I can see he's a right little charmer, just like me.'

'Yep. You win that one, hands down.' Her smile sagged a little, and Kieran was reminded that it was his charm that had ultimately led to one night of passion and this little boy.

Seamus yawned, and Kieran felt his heart swell. Gently he cuddled his warm bundle against his chest. Shock banged through him. Whatever his feelings about love and father-hood, he wouldn't be able to walk away from this family and never look back. It was way too late for that. He was going to be looking over his shoulder for the rest of his life.

CHAPTER FOUR

ABBY dropped onto the lumpy couch in the lounge, holding Seamus tight, as though for protection, though what from she had no idea. Earlier in the day, at the airport, she'd felt like she could trust him to do the right thing, that he wouldn't turn their world upside down. That had been in direct contrast to the way she'd reacted to him. The deep pull in her stomach toward him had stunned her. She'd always known she still cared about this man but never had she considered how explosive those feelings might be. No wonder she felt in need of protection. From Kieran? Or from herself?

She glanced across at him wiping down the kitchen benches. Hard to believe he'd cooked dinner. No one did that for her. Not even her father. But Kieran had taken charge, preparing their meal while she'd dealt with the kids' food. She knew he'd needed something to keep himself occupied and avoid getting too involved in the children's night-time rituals. He'd watched her feeding Seamus from a safe distance, grimacing when mushy food had ended up on her T-shirt. He had a lot to learn. She called softly, 'Thanks for dinner, and especially thanks for cleaning up.'

He turned and gazed at her, that bewildered look that had appeared when he had first held Seamus still there. 'I don't know how you do this all the time.'

'Goes with the territory of being a mum. Don't feel sorry for me. I love it.'

'I can see that.' His gaze dropped to Seamus, and his expression became guarded. What was he thinking? Did he accept Seamus as a son? Or as another problem to be dealt with? When she'd placed the baby in his arms Kieran hadn't known what to do. Even the simple act of holding a child seemed to unsettle him, and when she'd refused to take Seamus back, stepping away from them, he had looked completely lost. Maybe she shouldn't have done that, but she'd sensed he would need some gentle pushing when it came to coping with the children.

She also sensed his vulnerability, and didn't

know what to do about it, didn't understand why he felt that way. There was a real possibility of making things worse, not better, unless he opened up and talked about what bothered him. Her stomach clenched. Was this really what she wanted? Kieran becoming involved in the family? Maybe she was setting something in motion that she'd later come to regret, something like having to move to Ireland so they could be closer to each other. A chill slipped over her skin. Leave home and cross to the other side of the world? No way. Not even for the children's sake.

But Olivia and Seamus needed him, needed to know him, and already they were further along that track than she'd expected they'd be on day one. Admittedly when she'd forced Kieran to keep holding Seamus he hadn't been happy, but neither had he protested. Had he thought that would make him appear weak? She hoped not. He wasn't a weak man in any sense. Holding his son for the very first time had to have had an effect on him, one she hoped he'd absorbed and found he enjoyed. She should be feeling thrilled that he'd not given into whatever had bothered him, but instead she felt rattled.

Throughout the long months of her pregnancy and over the fifteen months of being a single parent, she'd never experienced any loneliness, never worried that she mightn't cope. And yet now, with Kieran here in her home, she felt uncertain. She couldn't dispel the sensation of the ground sliding out from under her. Of her life being about to change radically. What if she'd made a mistake bringing Kieran into Olivia and Seamus' lives?

No. She shoved that selfish idea away. She might've done the wrong thing for her but it was right for them.

'Abigail, are you all right?' Kieran interrupted her swarming thoughts. 'You've gone awfully quiet.'

Shaking away her doubts, she tried for a deep breath and the strength to cope. 'Couldn't be better.' *Couldn't I?* These weird, mixed-up feelings would soon pass. They had to if she was to survive the next eight weeks. 'I'm going to put this guy to bed, or he'll be grizzly all day tomorrow.'

So would she if she didn't get a decent night's sleep. She'd lain awake for hours last night, worrying about Kieran's arrival. Tonight she'd just sleep. He was here, and whatever happened would happen, and she could deal with it later. Yeah, right. Who was she kidding?

Kieran watched her with that perceptive gleam in his eyes. If he could read her mind, he'd be as confused as she was. She shrugged. 'I won't be long. Make yourself comfortable.'

But not too comfortable. This is my castle, the one place in the world I usually feel safe from everything and everyone. You could so easily destroy that for me by becoming too involved with us. By making my heart remember how close I came to falling in love with you in Dublin. At the end of your term here you'll go back and leave me with your scent touching my furnishings, my clothes. Your presence will fill the corners, sit at the table, take over my kitchen.

'I'll make us some tea. Or do you prefer coffee?' Kieran still watched her.

'Tea, thanks.' See, they didn't even know the most basic things about each other. Her face warmed. But they did have an intimate knowledge of each other. As the warmth became hot she fled the room, needing to put space between her and the man who'd made love to her so thoroughly she could still remember every detail two years later.

Singing a lullaby as she tucked Seamus under the cotton covers, the peace that usually stole over her at this moment wasn't forthcoming. Within a few hours Kieran had taken that from her. How much more would he take before he left? Would she survive intact? Would her heart cope? And she'd thought the hardest part of this visit would be the issues surrounding the children. How stupid of her.

'You're singing like an Irish mam.' Kieran spoke softly from the doorway. 'I like that.'

Abby's heart leapt. 'Don't creep up on me like that.' Then she focused on what he'd said. 'Did your mother sing to you?'

'Yeah…' The word whispered across his lips. 'I remember her singing to Morag more than me, but I know I got the same when I was little.'

'What happened to your mother?' No one had ever mentioned her, not even Morag.

'Unbeknown to anyone, she had diabetes. Our father came home one night to find her in a coma on the bathroom floor. She never recovered.'

'Kieran, I'm so sorry.' Her heart squeezed for him. 'How old were you?'

'Four.' There was a lot of pain behind that single word.

'I certainly know how hard losing a mother is, but at least I was an adult.' Not that it had made it any easier, but at least she had been able to understand some of the process.

Kieran stepped into the centre of the room. Of her bedroom. What had happened to making her a cup of tea? Had he been drawn to Seamus instead?

He asked, 'Why does Seamus sleep in here?'

'Because Olivia has the only other bedroom. I don't want Seamus disturbing her when he wakes during the night.'

Tucking the blue cotton blanket around a very sleepy boy, she didn't have to look up to know Kieran was studying the room with its bright red and white curtains and bedspread.

'Hardly ideal. What about some privacy for yourself?'

'There is no such thing as privacy when you have two small children, believe me.' Neither was there a need. It wasn't like she had someone special in her life to share this room with. Her eyes lifted to Kieran. The moisture in her mouth dried. An image of them in bed together filled her head. Trying to shake it away, she swore silently. Kieran would not become that special person. No man would. Hadn't she learned her lesson well?

'Surely you must want to take a break from the children at times?'

'I work so I already get a break.' Did he think the kids were too much for her? She managed very well, thank you. 'Dad helps by taking them over to his house sometimes.' And she began another lullaby.

He didn't say any more, instead wandered over to stand beside her, looking down at Seamus. What did he see? His family likeness? Did he look at Seamus as his son? Her singing dwindled to a halt. It was hard to sing with Kieran standing so close she could feel the heat from his body. She also felt self-conscious. She didn't exactly have a fantastic voice.

Seamus half-heartedly waved a fist at her. Or was it at Kieran? Glancing sideways, she studied Kieran watching Seamus. His hands were jammed into his pockets, and he stood with his legs slightly apart. What she wouldn't give to know what was going on in that head of his.

Reaching into the cot to run the back of her

hand over Seamus's warm, soft cheek, her heart squeezed. Her precious, little boy. She loved him so much she could cry. Kieran had missed out on lots already, which was entirely her fault. A fact she readily acknowledged.

Kieran had surprised her by being nervous when he'd first seen Olivia. There'd been something akin to fear in his eyes, and vulnerability. As though he'd felt completely out of his depth. His movements had been stilted, as though he'd never held a child before. And then he'd had to hold *his* child for the first time. She'd thought he'd be very much in control of the situation, of his emotions. From what she knew of him, he usually was.

What about when they'd made love? If that had shown controlled emotions then she was a possum. Her skin tingled at the memory of that night. Never before had she known anything like it. Making love with Kieran had spoiled her for ever. There wouldn't be another man on earth who'd measure up. Which perfectly suited her plan to remain forever single.

Seamus's eyes closed, blinked open. 'The little monkey's fighting going to sleep.' Abby smiled, first at Seamus then at Kieran, who still kept a closed expression on his face. 'He does that every night. It's like he doesn't want to miss out on anything.'

'Does he sleep right through the night?'

'Most of the time.'

From down the hall Olivia called, 'Abby, Teddy's got his foot stuck in a drawer.'

Abby chuckled. 'I'd better go and sort this out as Olivia won't go to sleep without Teddy.'

Kieran watched her leave the bedroom, totally unfazed by the children's demands. Damn, but she was good with them. A natural mother. Warmth stole over him. The kids were extremely lucky. He turned back to the boy, who'd finally succumbed to sleep, one fist pressed against his mouth, the other flung above his head. Kieran leaned forward, reached in and ran the back of his hand over Seamus's cheek, as he'd seen Abby do earlier. The warmth grew as Seamus's soft skin seemed to melt against his harsher skin. Beautiful.

Scary. He tugged his hand away, straightened. His body cooled. He couldn't do this. He didn't have Abby's knack with children. Abby didn't just feed Seamus, she fed him with love. She didn't bath Olivia, she bathed her with devotion.

He didn't know how to comfort, to play. It wasn't in him to cherish another human.

Doctoring was about fixing, not nurturing. He didn't know where he'd start if he had to take care of this little man even for an hour or two. Just standing here, he felt responsible for Seamus and that didn't sit comfortably.

The earlier panic began rising again. He could not become involved with Olivia and Seamus, become a part of this family. It would take a wet day in hell before he'd be ready for that. Or capable of doing what was expected of him.

Abby heard the phone ringing in the kitchen and wondered which of her sisters that might be. Stephanie's voice bubbled down the line. 'Hey, Abby, how's things? How's the great man from Ireland? All excited to see Olivia?'

Abby dredged up a laugh. 'Olivia dazzled him.' Which was certainly more than she'd managed.

'I bet she did.'

'She chattered nonstop to him, but wouldn't let him bath her.' Much to Kieran's relief.

'I bet Seamus won him over in an instant.'

'No. That's a work in progress.' Neither of her sisters knew who Seamus's dad was, but they probably had their suspicions. Anyone could do the sum and they'd both known there hadn't been anyone else in her life since Phillip had turned out to be such a rat. Now was probably the time to tell them, but she'd wait until she knew what Kieran would do.

Thankfully Steph changed the subject. 'I bought a new dress today for a party I'm going to. Can you take the hem up for me?'

What ever happened to 'do you mind?' or 'please'? Abby sighed. What did she expect? She'd always done alterations for her sisters. 'Bring it round on Saturday morning.'

Sometimes she felt Charlie and Steph didn't even consider she might have a life of her own. Certainly neither realised how time-consuming bringing up two very young children could be. What would they say if she left the children with them for a day and went out shopping, visiting the beauty parlour or just lying on a lounger, reading a magazine? She couldn't help the small smile that twisted her mouth. They'd be horrified. As far as Steph was concerned, children definitely didn't go with the image of a lawyer in one of the city's top firms. Neither did Charlie think hotshot real estate salespeople should have kids clinging to their tailored suits. But they loved their niece and nephew, and her. As she loved them.

Six years younger than her, her sisters had always turned to her for help with things since the day she'd come home to nurse their mother. When their mum had died she'd kept right on looking out for them. At twenty-three they didn't really need her to do that now, but she wouldn't have it any other way. Most of the time.

Stephanie was saying, 'I wonder if Kieran would like to go to the party. The girls from the office would love him, especially with that divine accent. His gorgeous looks won't hurt either.'

Abby's stomach plummeted. She knew Kieran loved parties. Her brother had often talked about all the socialising they'd done together. Why shouldn't he go? He was a free agent. Because he'd come here to work, it didn't mean he had to be a saint for the duration of his stay. What he did in his spare time had nothing to do with her. He'd probably be glad of a distraction from the 'children' problem.

'Is Kieran still there? I'd like to talk to him.'

'Sure.' But then she heard a car starting. At her front gate? Kieran? A low, throaty engine roared away. A sports car kind of sound. Definitely Kieran. 'Seems I'm wrong. He's just left.'

Without a word. Whatever happened to saying goodnight? Anger vied with disappointment. Surely she wasn't asking too much? Even if he couldn't handle being a dad, he could've poked his head around the corner and said something before he disappeared. Even if the situation had got too much for him and he'd needed to get away, how hard would that have been? Guess she didn't rate too highly on his list of important people or things. Her shoulders slumped. Was she being impatient? Probably. But she didn't know how to be any different.

Stephanie didn't seem too concerned. 'I'll catch up with him later. I'll bring my dress over on Friday. See you.' Click. She'd gone, too.

Leaving Abby feeling incredibly lonely. At home with two children while their other parent, as such, raced back to town and presumably the safety of his new apartment. So where was the problem? She hadn't expected him to make himself so comfortable that he'd stay to start taking over caring for the children. *Give the guy a chance to get used to all this.*

Two mugs stood on the bench. The kettle was

warm to her touch. So he'd got that far with making the drinks. She boiled the water again and took her tea with her to check up on Seamus. Sound asleep, he looked angelic, which he was. Most of the time. A smile tugged at her mouth, despite her gloomy mood. Seamus always did this to her whenever she was out of sorts. One look and she felt better about her world.

Now she studied his face, so like the face that had haunted her over the last two years. Moving away, she sank onto the end of her bed, her thoughts automatically returning to Kieran. Today, when she'd met him at the airport, she'd seen that her memory had been correct. The sharp lines running down the sides of his mouth were still there, as was that lopsided smile that sliced through her every time. Those full lips that had done untold exciting things to her body were exactly as she recalled. Oh, yes, her body remembered him very well.

Too well. Now all she had to do was cope with him being around for two months when just looking at him sent all her hormones into a dance. That was all. *That was all?*

CHAPTER FIVE

DRESSED in non-matching panties and bra, Abby headed down the hall, vigorously towelling her freshly washed hair. How could she have slept in? How had she managed to sleep at all with everything going on in her mind? Mainly things about Kieran. He really had got to her in a very short time. She had to get herself under control, stop thinking Kieran at every turn.

Seamus played with a wooden truck in the bedroom, damp nappies drooping around his knees. She left him to go and start making toast. Olivia was chattering in the kitchen, probably telling Teddy what she wanted for breakfast. Had she dressed herself this morning? Some days she did so, with bizarre results, some days she wanted Abby to do it.

At the kitchen door Abby lowered the towel, looking for Olivia, and gasped. Her heart stopped, then with a thud resumed its regular beat.

'Kieran. What are you doing here? How did you get in?' Hadn't she locked up before going to bed last night?

'Good morning, Abigail.' He looked past her. For Seamus? Surely that had to be a good sign?

'Morning yourself,' she muttered, then realised where his gaze had settled and hurriedly draped the towel around her body. Except the towel was too small and only covered from her breasts to halfway down her backside. Abby started backing out of the kitchen. She'd get dressed properly before asking why he was here.

'I opened the door,' Olivia informed her importantly.

'Haven't I told you not to open the door to strangers?' Abby hesitated in mid-flight and eyed Olivia sternly.

Kieran explained, his gaze now in the vicinity of her face, 'You can blame me. When I knocked and got no answer I came round to the window to see if you were about. Olivia saw me and let me in. There are advantages to being Uncle Kieran.' At last his eyes met hers, twinkling at her. 'Anyway, I'd hope I wasn't a stranger.'

She knew he was referring to his relationship with her, not Olivia. She stuttered, 'W-what b-brings you out here this early?'

'I wanted to apologise for my abrupt departure last night. It was rude of me.' He raised his hands and shrugged disarmingly. 'I admit to being a little overwhelmed. Throw in exhaustion after that damned flight and everything caught up with me in a hurry. But I should've said good-night.'

'Apology accepted.' He surprised her, admitting he'd been out of his depth. But right now she had to feed and clothe the kids, then get to work on time. No, first she had to get dressed before Kieran began sizing her up again in his toe-curling way.

He said, 'I thought it best to see you before we get to work. It might be a bit awkward explaining in front of other people.'

'Work?' He was joking, right? 'You're not starting today?' She'd been relying on having a few more days before he invaded her work space as well as her home.

'Might as well. There's nothing else on my agenda at the moment, and I understand Michael is already on leave.'

'His son's desperately ill and last week they got word of a liver that might be compatible in Brisbane.'

'Then the sooner I start, the better. Let's hope the operation on his son is successful.'

'Everyone's got their fingers crossed for that,' Abby responded. 'We've seen the pain the family is suffering.'

'I can't imagine being in their shoes.' Kieran turned for the back door. 'I'll see you later on.'

Relieved that he was leaving, she couldn't explain the little gremlin that made her say, 'Since you're here, can you put the kettle on and start making toast? I'm already running late and could do with a hand.'

He slowly turned back into the room, his eyes again roaming over her. The playboy was definitely to the fore this morning, not the overwhelmed man trying to deal with two very small relatives he couldn't quite fathom. 'Of course. Where do you keep everything?'

'Fridge, cupboard and pantry.' Abby beat a hasty retreat to her bedroom.

As she changed Seamus into shorts and T-shirt she could hear Olivia telling Kieran what she wanted on her toast and what Seamus liked, and that she wanted juice. 'No, not in that glass. The other one.'

Then, 'Abby doesn't cut our toast like that. She makes it into squares.' And, 'Not that runny honey. It falls off the toast and messes Seamus's shirt.'

Abby grinned in sympathy for Kieran. He was learning breakfast wasn't as straightforward as he'd previously believed.

Time to rescue the man. Back in the kitchen she placed Seamus in his highchair and put his toast in front of him before grinning at Kieran. 'I heard you getting your instructions from little miss bossy britches.'

Kieran placed a mug of tea on the table in front of her. 'I never knew making toast could be so difficult. I hope your tea is to your satisfaction?' He grinned back before looking over to the highchair.

His eyes fixed on Seamus poking food into his mouth and over his cheeks. A mask of indifference hid whatever he truly felt about his little boy and the situation he found himself in. Were his feelings good ones? Or did he still want nothing to do with the kids? Her heart squeezed for

Kieran and Seamus. They needed time together, lots of it.

Seamus dropped a piece of toast on the floor. Wrong way up, of course. And Kieran grimaced. It didn't seem to register with him there was a mess to clean up.

Abby grabbed a dishcloth and wiped the floor. He mightn't have leapt in to do it but looking at Olivia's jam-covered toast now cut into squares, albeit very large ones, he seemed to be getting the hang of breakfast under his niece's tutelage.

Abby asked cheekily, 'Do I get any toast?'

Kieran dragged his eyes around to her. 'Coming up. Squares or oblongs? Jam or honey?'

'Definitely squares and jam. What about you? Have you eaten?'

He ran a hand over his chin. 'I think I've just gone off toast. I'll head away to ED in a moment.'

Abby grinned to hide the flutter in her tummy. He looked totally unlike the perfectly turned-out doctor with a streak of jam now decorating his chin. She reached over with a paper towel and wiped it clean. 'Rule number one with children. Never go out before checking in the mirror. You'll be surprised what you might find.'

Something like horror filled his eyes and he quickly checked his immaculate, crease-free shirt front, flicking a crumb off his tie.

She laughed. 'Relax. You've managed to stay clean despite everything. Now go. I've got to get these two ready.'

'Now who's the bossy britches?' he muttered.

'You're welcome to stay and help some more.'

'I think not. You make it look so easy and I'm learning it's not.'

'I've had more practice,' she quipped without thought to the ramifications.

'To be sure, and whose fault is that?'

Tea splashed over her hand as she jolted from the shock of his suddenly harsh tone. So, Kieran's good mood had been a facade. And the guilt she'd tamped down overnight swamped her again. He would never forgive her.

Abby dashed into ED, pretending to herself she wasn't looking out for Kieran. She wanted to avoid him for a while if at all possible. For the whole day would be better but that would be asking too much. 'Hi, Sally, sorry I'm late but it was a disaster zone at my house this morning.'

That had to be the understatement of the century. For some inexplicable reason Olivia had demanded that she stay home with Grandad instead of going to the crèche workers. Abby had delivered one very grumpy little girl to the crèche. Thank goodness Seamus seemed happy enough to be there with his little friends. At least Kieran had left before all the fuss had started. It might've kept him away permanently. She sighed. She was being unfair again.

All the way to work she'd thought about him, how his usual confidence had been undermined by the children. Would he have coped better if it had only been Olivia he'd had to contend with? Was it because of finding himself a father that he was outside his comfort zone?

Sally tossed a file on the desk in front of Abby. 'I thought you might've given our new boss a lift to work for his first day since he's part of your family.'

Abby dropped onto a chair. She'd given the guy dinner, a son and probably a headache. She didn't need to give him anything else. 'I don't think he'd be happy squashed into my car among car seats and kids.' Or within touching distance of her.

Sally grinned at her. 'Here I was hoping Dr

Flynn might not have gone to his new apartment last night.'

Abby snatched the file up and jerked it open. 'I know. You only want to see me happily married.' They'd had this conversation so often Abby knew the lines off by heart. 'Do me a big favour, drop the whole Kieran thing. For ever.'

One thing for sure, Kieran seemed to have way too many hang-ups when it came to family and commitment for her to consider him for the role of husband. But Sally didn't know the score and Abby just couldn't bring herself to explain. The tension in the back of her head wound tighter.

'For now.' Sally looked around the department. 'Can you give Barbara a hand?'

'Sure.' Something other than Kieran to focus on.

'But where is Dr Flynn? I'd have thought he'd be the type to always be early.' Sally flipped through some files, her gaze fixed somewhere out in the department.

Abby shook her head at her friend. This was what Kieran did so well; how he got everyone in a twitter. Then she saw Sally's eyes widen and her mouth slide into a beautiful smile. And she knew without looking around that Kieran had arrived. If he could do this to a sane, married woman, what chance did anyone else have?

What chance did she have?

She turned and faced him, but he was too busy introducing himself to Pete and Rose to see her. The interns were drinking up every word Kieran uttered. 'Making fools of themselves,' she muttered.

Damn but the man knew how to work a scene. She looked to Sally for some sanity and was sadly disappointed. 'Stop drooling, it doesn't suit you.'

'Why not? Everyone else is.' Sally grinned. 'Look at those eyes, that body. Are you sure I'm married?' Then she nudged Abby. 'You've got a patient. And if I didn't know better I'd say you were interested in Dr Charming. Why else are you still hanging around the station?'

She wouldn't lower herself to answer. If only Sally knew the half of it. Kieran hid so much behind those twinkling eyes. He gave away nothing of last night's turmoil at meeting his son for the first time. Laughter carried across the department and caused Abby's stomach to roll over agonisingly. She had to admire his nerve. His world had been rocked right off its axis and no one watching him now would ever guess how he felt about that.

'Hey, Abby, Darren Shore's here again. He's had a wee disagreement with his skateboard.' Barbara took care as she helped a lad onto the bed in a cubicle.

'Hi, Darren, Jim.' Abby nodded at the weary man already slouching in the chair on the other side of the bed. 'Can't trust those skateboards not to want to go their own way.' Abby noted Darren's careful movements. 'Where does it hurt?'

'Here.' Darren tapped his wrist gingerly. 'And here.'

The ulna. Two breaks? Or transferred pain? Abby carefully slid the sleeve of Darren's shirt up and felt the swelling of his wrist. A massive bruise covered most of his arm. 'We'll send you for an X-ray after I get a doctor to look at you and sign a form. First we'll clean you up, see how much skin you've removed. What did you crash into this time?'

'The concrete wall by the school gates.'

'Guess you came off worse than the wall, then.'

'Yeah. Ouch.' The boy sucked in a mouthful of air.

'Let's give you some Entonox to take away the pain and make you feel happy.' Abby handed Darren a mouthpiece attached to tubing leading from a gas tank. 'Take a deep breath of that every time your arm hurts. I think you need a stitch or two in your head to stop the bleeding.' A large bruise had formed there.

Barbara slipped out of the cubicle, saying, 'I'll go find a doctor.'

Darren squinted up at Abby. 'Is my arm really broken? I'll still be able to ride my board, won't I?'

'No, you won't.' Darren's father spoke for the first time. 'That damned board can go in the rubbish. I'm tired of you coming off it and hurting yourself. There's not a day goes by that you're not covered in bruises.'

More bruises? Abby glanced at Darren's legs but he wore jeans.

'Dad, no. You can't throw my board away.' All pain was momentarily forgotten as Darren sat up and glared at his parent. 'Gramps gave it to me for my birthday and he'll go bonkers if you take it off me. It's a really expensive one with the best wheels you can get.'

Jim growled, 'I'll deal with your grandfather. Believe me, that board is trash.'

Abby gently pushed Darren back against the pillow. 'Let's get you patched up, and worry about the board later.'

'I'm going home to hide it.' But Darren's bravado quickly evaporated as pain struck again.

Abby began swabbing the cut on Darren's head, noting an older bruise above his eye. An earlier skating accident? 'Do you wear protective gear? Like a helmet, for starters?'

'Yes. Dad won't let me go out without it.'

'He's right. You don't want to injure your head.' Abby noticed purple swelling on the uninjured arm. 'Darren, I want to remove your jeans and examine your legs.'

His father growled, 'Spends more time falling off than actually riding the damned skateboard.'

Abby could sympathise with both of them. Darren was obviously full of spirits and not put off by his accidents, but what parent would be happy about always taking their child to get stitched up? She'd hate seeing Seamus or Olivia hurt. She might be hiding the skateboard, too, despite knowing life was about getting out there and taking risks.

Taking risks? Like she did? The biggest risk she'd taken since getting engaged to Phillip had been flying to Ireland for the funerals. Then her grief had been so crippling she hadn't thought about dealing with Customs and Immigration and all the things people had warned her about. She'd just clung to her sisters and followed the arrows.

The cubicle curtains swished open, revealing a confident Kieran with a boggle-eyed Barbara in tow. Another victim. Careful, or you'll be dribbling. Abby sighed. As if she could talk. From the moment she'd met Kieran she'd fallen under his spell. Even if he hadn't been so good looking and sexy, he only had to open his mouth and speak in that lyrical accent and her knees weakened.

'I hear some stitches are required.' Kieran spoke into the sudden quiet.

There, just as she'd thought. The Irish lilt. Her knees were ready to dump her on the floor, despite her wariness of him. 'Darren, this is Dr Flynn. Darren's one of our regulars. I'm just going to get his file. I want to check on something. Barbara can assist you, Doctor.'

His brow creased but he didn't try to stop her

leaving the cubicle that felt as small as a kennel with five people crammed in there. Especially with Kieran present, all the air seemed to have disappeared. She needed to put space between them before she became a brainless ninny. She'd better get over herself. And especially get over Kieran. At least the accusatory tone Kieran had directed as he'd left her house had gone, no doubt put aside for a more suitable time.

Darren's file lay in the in-tray at the nurses' station. Sinking onto a chair, she read through the notes recording a previous broken arm, and on three separate occasions he'd had cuts requiring stitches. No mention of bruising. So why the excessive bruising today? Her heart slowed. She didn't like to think about what the sudden onset of severe bruising could mean.

Pete sat down beside her to write up notes on his patient. Peering at her file, he asked, 'Why are you interested in that?'

'That Darren's file?' Kieran asked from above her.

'Yes.' How had she missed his approach? She thought she had extra-supersensory feelings whenever Kieran was around. Looking up, she saw him watching her intently. What did he see?

Someone suitable to bring up his niece? And his son? Or a woman who he'd once enjoyed a few special hours with? What did he remember of that night in Dublin?

'Are you worried about Darren? You seem a little distracted.'

Of course she was distracted. Who wouldn't be in the circumstances? With a flick of her ponytail she focused on their patient.

'I'm not sure. Darren falls off his skateboard a lot. But I can't find any record here of severe bruising associated with previous injuries. He's got bruises in more places than I'd expect from this morning's accident.'

Pete said, 'He's a boy. Of course he's always falling off and getting bruised. Nothing sinister there.'

But Kieran took her doubts seriously. 'Are you worried that there might be a medical cause?'

'Yes. I think we should be investigating further.' She didn't go as far as to say what tests she'd do if it was up to her. Occasionally even she knew when to keep quiet.

Pete muttered, 'If Dr Flynn has checked him out, why are you concerned?'

'Abigail has a valid point. Darren's bruising is

abnormal. It doesn't hurt to take another look. Better to find she's wrong than send the boy away with an illness we overlooked. Always listen to your staff. They see things you might not.'

Abby knew Pete would give her a hard time about this later, but it felt good to have her concerns taken seriously. After all, she did have some knowledge about these things.

'I'm going to take a blood sample from Darren. Clotting factors and a blood count. Is that what you had in mind?' Kieran cocked an eyebrow at her.

'Yes. But I hope I'm wrong about the diagnosis I'm considering.'

Unfortunately she wasn't. The lab rang within an hour.

'Darren has leukaemia.' Kieran's jaw tightened. 'We're sending him to Day Stay for a pathologist to do a bone-marrow aspiration to determine the type.'

Abby's heart squeezed for Darren and his father. Their lives were about to be turned upside down and inside out. Their situation was unimaginable for any parent.

'I'd better go and tell Jim.' Kieran stood as

though glued to the floor. His hand dragged down his cheek. 'I hate this part of the job.' Then he muttered something like, 'And today it seems worse.'

'Want me to come with you? Or sit with Darren while you take his father to your office?' Abby didn't know how she'd cope if anyone ever had to tell her something as devastating about Seamus or Olivia.

'How does a parent deal with this?' Kieran croaked.

She shivered. 'Let's hope we never have to find out.'

Telling Jim Shore that his fun-loving son was gravely ill and needed more tests had been one of the hardest things Kieran had ever had to do.

For some inexplicable reason young Darren's plight rocked him on a deep personal level. For the first time during his career as an emergency specialist the sense of regret and pain for his patient felt too close. He couldn't understand his feelings, but they were very real. He'd always found this side of his job hard but today was especially difficult.

Other patients awaiting his attention gave him

a much-needed distraction. But later, when the pathologist phoned down as a matter of courtesy to tell him that the bone-marrow results showed acute lymphoblastic leukaemia, Kieran's head spun. Even though he'd been expecting the result, he found it difficult to accept. He'd known what the initial results meant. But Darren was a child, a happy boy full of life.

Just like Seamus. What if something like this happened to his little boy? Would he survive the pain of watching his son becoming extremely ill? How did a man cope as he watched his child being put through intensive and painful treatment?

Abby touched his shoulder lightly. 'Are you all right? I saw you on the phone.'

He shook his head. 'That was the pathologist confirming Darren has ALL.'

Sadness and horror filled Abby's eyes before she quickly turned away, murmuring, 'These are the days I hate my job.'

'I know what you mean.' But today felt worse than ever before. Today he understood on a deeper level what Jim Shore might be feeling. And it was sure to be a lot worse than Kieran could imagine. A band of pain throbbed in the back of his head.

Abby said, 'I feel like rushing to the crèche and hugging the kids tight, to reassure myself they're fine and that nothing can touch them.'

'A natural response, I'd have thought.' He squeezed her hand before moving away. 'Take five to go and see them.'

'Are you sure?' Her eyes widened. Surprised he could be so understanding?

'Absolutely.' Well, he surprised himself at his sense of helplessness right now. The only thing he could think to do was send Abby to see the children.

Her smile was thanks enough. 'Come with me. Seeing the kids might make you feel a bit better.'

He shook his head. 'No, I'm needed here.' As head of the department, how would it look to the staff if he went charging off to see his niece just because of the diagnosis on one of his patients? Damn it, they'd be sending him home in no time at all.

He tried not to watch Abby as she raced away. The ultimate mother with all the right instincts. Could he even come close to that as an uncle or father? Vulnerability squeezed his gut. Sweat pricked his skin. Despite his denials, those two children were already overtaking his determination to remain aloof.

Did that mean he'd begun accepting he had a son? With all the connotations of what that meant? No. It was far too soon for him to be ready. He would never be ready. But the control he had over his life was rapidly becoming a myth.

HOPE. The sign flashed by, and this time Kieran didn't even slow down. He didn't know why the compulsion to see Olivia and Seamus felt so strong, didn't understand the need to reassure himself they were healthy and happy.

To be sure, he knew they were all of those things and more. But he had to *see* for himself. His hands gripped the steering-wheel, stones flicked up as he braked hard outside Abby's cottage. Abby. How did he explain his mad rush from town at nine o'clock at night? She'd think he'd gone crazy.

But it was almost as though she'd expected him if the lack of surprise in those expressive eyes was anything to go by. 'Hey, want a coffee? I've just made a plunger full.'

'That would be lovely. But don't move. I'll get it.'

What was really lovely was Abby. Her legs were curled under her bottom as she sat in an old rocker on the veranda. A magazine lay open on her lap, her hair spilling around her face, her hands lightly holding her mug. Her soft mouth relaxed into a welcoming smile. The efficient, serious nurse he'd worked beside that day had been put away for the night.

'Thanks. You know where everything is. I'm catching the last of the sun now that the kids are asleep.'

His heart lurched. Disappointment warred with relief. Olivia and Seamus were asleep. He could take a quick peek and get out of here. Forget the coffee. It would keep him awake half the night anyway.

Olivia slept under a light sheet, lying on her back with Teddy clasped to her side in a headlock. Her curls dark against her pale Irish skin. Kieran leaned against the doorframe and watched her. Again he was stunned at the likeness to his sister. Looking at Olivia felt like Morag was still with him. He wanted to talk to his sister, tell her he missed her, explain that

Olivia was gorgeous, happy and well cared-for and that she mustn't worry about her.

Kieran shut his eyes, squeezed the bridge of his nose. He could not be tearing up. Not now, not when he'd done his grieving two years earlier. He'd come out here to see the children, not to let the past grip him in a wave of nostalgia. He blinked, sniffed. And stepped up to the bed, bent over and kissed Olivia's forehead. Softly.

'Thank goodness you're safe,' he whispered.

As he straightened up he noticed the collage of photos adorning one of the walls. Morag. David. Olivia. The three of them in different poses— laughing, serious, waving, playing. In the half-light from the doorway Kieran studied every photo thoroughly, his heart feeling as though it was breaking. It was wrong for those two to have died. Abby was doing her best to make up for Olivia's loss but the child would never really know her real parents.

He turned to gaze at his niece again. And fought off the tears once more. 'Goodnight, little one.'

He backed quietly out of the room. He'd just take a quick look in on Seamus and go.

Seamus was a restless sleeper. His feet moved

almost continuously, and his hands plucked at the sheet, pulling it in every direction. His stuffed toy, a monkey, lay on the floor. He looked so like the Flynns with his colouring and features that Kieran's heart swelled. With pride? Not likely. How could he be proud of a child he didn't want to acknowledge? He didn't mean the biological ownership. He was definitely this little guy's dad in that respect.

But Abby was a part of Seamus, too. It showed in his easygoing temperament, his enquiring mind and gurgling laugh.

This is a one-year-old. How can you possibly tell so much about his personality at that age? You're looking for things in the kid, making them up as you go along.

Was he? Kieran's hands fisted in his pockets and he rolled on and off the balls of his feet while his gaze never left the infant. Looking for more characteristics to attribute to Abby? Making Seamus more of a Brown than a Flynn? Pushing the kid further away? Trying to justify himself when moments ago he'd thought it a tragedy that Olivia didn't know her parents?

But Seamus had met him, would always know him, albeit distantly. In this case, that was best for Seamus. Far, far better than being hurt by lack of love.

He bit his upper lip. Time to go. The children were as happy and healthy as he'd expect them to be. Abby made sure of that as far as it was humanly possible. As a doctor he understood nothing could be done to prevent a tragedy such as Darren Shore's occurring. As an uncle he felt there had to be something he could do. As a parent? A hollow feeling in the pit of his gut gave him no answers. Except to make him feel worse than ever.

It was impossible to leave. His feet were glued to the floor as he watched Seamus sleeping. When he did finally leave the cramped bedroom Abby had moved inside to watch television and darkness had settled outside.

'Everything okay?' Abby asked as he hesitated in her lounge doorway.

'Exactly as I'd expected.' Except for his own messy emotions, which weren't listening to him when he tried to take control and get on with what he'd come here for. To run an emergency department.

CHAPTER SIX

IT SEEMED Kieran couldn't stay away. Surprising Abby, he turned up at the cottage on Friday after work moments after Steph and her boyfriend, Andrew, arrived.

Olivia charged him down as he stepped onto the small veranda, insisting he pick her up. He hesitated before bending to swing her up into his arms. Olivia giggled nonstop. Her vise-like grip around his neck made him wince. But at least he was playing the game and trying to please his niece.

Abby grinned. 'Guess you'll be wanting a beer, too.'

'Sure thing.' Kieran turned to Steph and gave her an awkward hug with Olivia stuck between them. 'It's great to see you again. Is Charlie here, too?'

'Not yet, but I'm sure she won't be far away.' Steph turned to Andrew and made the introductions.

Abby dragged out the stack of hard plastic deck chairs from the laundry.

'Let me take those,' Kieran said from behind her.

She nearly leapt off the floor. She hadn't heard him following her. 'Thanks.' She could get used to having someone do things for her.

He carefully put Olivia down and picked up the stack with ease, then asked in a nonchalant tone, 'Where's Seamus?'

Yes! He'd asked after his son. Triumph spurted through Abby. A very small step but, in her book, a step nonetheless. 'With Dad, shifting the irrigation pump.'

'He's quite the little man, isn't he?' Kieran commented, and carried the chairs out to the veranda. 'Where's that beer? A man could die of thirst around here.'

Abby watched Kieran as he separated the chairs and passed them around. He was totally at ease, very different from the serious professional she worked with during the day. A bit like herself, she supposed. As he tipped a bottle to his lips her stomach muscles cramped. He was so darned sexy. To say nothing about his good looks. No wonder she'd never forgotten that night with him. He'd marked her for life.

What did he see when he looked at her? A harried mother and aunt? He wouldn't be impressed with the shapeless clothes she wore to hide what Phillip had often derisively called her fat body.

Those soul-destroying words still hurt. Words that had finished off any desire for marriage or even a long-term relationship. Phillip had dashed her trust completely, making her wise up to the dangers of falling in love. Like Kieran, he'd been charming and fun to be with initially. Then the snide comments about her body shape, her clothes, her hair, her everything had begun. Finding him in bed with her then closest friend had shattered her. Within twenty-four hours she'd returned home, taking nothing with her except a broken heart. And a wedding to cancel.

'Hope there's a cold one for me,' her dad called out as he came through the orchard, swinging Seamus down from his shoulders. 'It's got to be thirty degrees out here.'

Abby watched as Seamus headed straight for Kieran. The surprise on Kieran's face was a nice change from his usual wariness. Then Seamus grabbed at Kieran's knee-length shorts with his grubby hands, and she laughed out loud. 'Hope they're not your best pair.'

His smile was wry, but at least he did smile. 'They are now my "meet Seamus" pair.'

He might be way out of his comfort zone but he was trying, and that pleased her, eased some of the permanent tension making her edgy these days. If he kept this up, soon he'd be a part of the Brown clan, always welcome, always included in the happenings of the family.

But she had to remember not to get any closer to him. He might be the father of her son, but that's as far as it could go. As far as she could afford to let it go. *So there, hormones, behave. Concentrate on helping Kieran learn to love the children. Forget everything else.*

A car pulled up on the roadside and Charlie appeared, carrying a grocery bag. 'Hi, everyone. Hope you're hungry, I've got a ton of steak and sausages here.'

These were the nights Abby loved, when all her family got together for an impromptu meal. Seamus followed her as she headed into the kitchen to make a salad and put potatoes into the oven to bake.

'Don't you ever stop working?' Kieran

asked from the doorway, a frown crinkling his forehead.

'I gave the maid the night off,' she quipped, refusing to take his question seriously.

'Anything I can do?'

'You could see if anyone wants another drink.' Just then Seamus tugged the bottle opener from the table. 'That's my boy. Give it to Daddy.'

Kieran gasped. 'What did you say?'

The air whooshed out of her lungs. Where had that come from? She'd intended discussing with Kieran what she should call him when talking to Seamus before she mentioned the D word. She stared at Kieran aghast. He looked as shocked as she felt. 'I'm sorry. I shouldn't have said that. I…'

She spun around to the bench, staring at her shaking hands as she tried to pick up a knife to slice the tomatoes.

He'd never talk to her again. At least not for the rest of the evening even if he stayed now.

'Abby, it's all right.' Kieran's hand touched her shoulder, pressured her to turn to face him. 'I should have a name and I guess I am Seamus's father.'

Seamus bumped between their legs, startling

them both into looking down. He held the opener up to Kieran. Shock drained the colour from Kieran's cheeks. 'Did he really understand you? Does he know I'm his father?'

Kieran stared at his son, speechless. Then slowly crouched down and took the opener in one hand. He ran the other hand over Seamus's head, and whispered, 'Thanks, boyo.'

'Morning, Abigail. Late again, I see.' Kieran strode alongside her as she dashed down the corridor towards the department. His tone dampened her pleasure at seeing him.

'Only by five minutes.' At least she had a good excuse. 'Olivia tipped a bowl of porridge over herself and we had to start dressing all over again.' But, of course, he wouldn't know what that was like.

'Olivia must've looked a sight.' Kieran gave her a brief smile. 'But you must allow time for these things. It's not fair on your colleagues if you keep arriving late after the shift handover is under way.'

'Keep arriving late? I don't make a habit of it.'

'Twice last week.'

Who's counting? 'You really don't get it, do

you? Kids aren't that easy to organise.' How dared Kieran criticise her? She drew a breath. She hadn't finished. 'While you're at it, tell me where I'm supposed to find any extra time in the mornings. I'm already up by six, running around like a demented chook trying to get the house in order before my children strike.'

Kieran stared at her, amazed. 'Whoa, I only suggested you might try to be more punctual. Careful.' He grabbed her elbow and tugged her to one side as an orderly negotiated a bed past them. 'It's probably only a case of organising everything better.'

She jerked her arm free. The temptation to strangle him was huge. Had he not learned anything about raising children yet? Could he not try to understand how it was for her? 'Organised? Sure, buddy, from now on I'll get up at five, do the vacuuming, make the beds before Olivia and Seamus get out of them, prepare breakfast, hang out the washing in the dark, have my shower and put on make-up and immaculate clothes, and finally drive to work with two beautifully behaved children, beating the rush-hour traffic to arrive in the department all smiles and look-ing very serene.'

She sank back against the wall. What had got into her? Her tongue was like a runaway road-ster. It wasn't Kieran's fault she'd spent the week-end checking the gate to see if he might have turned up. She'd behaved worse than Olivia. Had he stayed away because of her stupid mistake of calling him Daddy on Friday night?

'Buddy?' Kieran stared at her as though she'd gone stark, raving mad. 'Abigail, is something wrong? I've obviously upset you.'

'Upset me?' Totally. Not because of his criti-cism but because he was never out of her head, keeping her awake hours after she went to bed every night. 'No, not at all. I've got a touch of Monday-itis.'

She spun around and headed for the nurses' station, Kieran keeping pace with her, thank-fully staying quiet.

'Abby, don't think you can ease your way in today. It's crazy around here already.' Sally added to her mounting stress. 'Kieran, cubicle three, please.'

Kieran reached for the file in Sally's hand. 'What have we got?'

'A twenty-five-year-old woman with an aching leg.'

'Abigail, come with me.'

Grrr. Abby wanted to go home and start again. To put on her best smile and pretend she was coping with Kieran reappearing in her life.

Reluctantly she followed him. He paused outside the cubicle, and his wary smile caught at her, undermining her bad mood. 'I apologise if I sound uncaring. I'm not. Guess this shows I don't know anything about parenting.'

She softened her tone. 'There's only one way to learn. It's called the hands-on approach.' A family could be a tie, and it hurt to know Kieran didn't want that.

'I know, and I should've visited over the weekend but I was busy.'

Sure, partying, socialising. Steph had told her he'd accepted her invitation to that party she'd mentioned. 'No rest for the wicked, eh?' Face it, Kieran could be very wicked. In the nicest, sexiest possible way, her brain mocked her.

A burly young man stood by the bed in the cubicle, his arm around the shoulders of a distressed woman. The obvious worry darkening his eyes made Abby take stock and push those distracting images of Kieran away. But she wished she had someone special to care for her as intensely. And she wasn't meaning her father or sisters.

Neither did she mean Kieran.

She was never going to get that close to the man. Or any other man, remember? *Remember?* Yes, she did. So why was she suddenly having all these odd feelings of missing out on something really important?

The young man said, 'It's Jane's right leg. She says it's agony to stand on. We can't get her jeans off, it's swollen so much.'

'Hello, Jane. I'm Dr Flynn and this is Nurse Brown. I am going to have to remove your jeans to examine your leg. We might have to use scissors.'

'I'll try pulling them off again.' Jane grimaced, but removing the jeans proved too painful.

'I guess there's no choice.' Abby went in search of scissors.

'I've only just bought these jeans,' Jane muttered when she returned.

Abby smiled in sympathy. 'They're gorgeous.'

Designer ones, the sort that Abby could never squeeze herself into. 'I bet you didn't get them here.'

'I bought them in Switzerland two weeks ago.'

Kieran's eyebrows rose fractionally. 'What were you doing there?'

'Skiing. Ahh…' The girl sucked a breath as the denim fell away, removing the pressure on the swelling.

'Any accidents or falls? You didn't twist your knee at any time?' Kieran queried as he examined the inflamed leg.

Jane shook her head. 'No, nothing like that.'

'When did you get back to New Zealand? Did you come straight through?' Abby asked, wondering if this could be a case of deep vein thrombosis. She looked up to find Kieran watching her. He nodded imperceptibly, as though to say she was on the right track.

'Two days ago. It's a long haul from Zurich, through Frankfurt, Hong Kong, Auckland. My body clock's only just catching up. I keep wanting to go to bed in the middle of the day.' Jane smiled for the first time. 'Not a good look when I'm supposed to be organising kayaking trips for tourists.'

'I'll bet.' Kieran smiled his big, calming smile.

That smile might not have had much effect on Jane, but it sent Abby's heart rate soaring. Fickle heart. She wasn't supposed to notice anything about Kieran other than his medical skills.

Next he asked, 'Any history of thrombosis in your family? Have you had a clot in the past?'

Tears welled in Jane's eyes. 'I wondered about that. I don't know of anyone having had clots but I'd have to ask Mum.'

Kieran said, 'Are you on an oral contraceptive?'

'Yes.'

'Did you take any aspirin before or during the flight?'

Jane shook her head. 'Will I be all right? People die of clots.'

'You've done the right thing coming in here.' Abby folded the now useless jeans.

Kieran explained what would happen next. 'I'll arrange an ultrasound scan of your veins. If that doesn't show up a clot, we'll X-ray the knee to see if you did some damage while skiing.'

Jane's lip trembled as she asked, 'Will I be all right? I mean, if it's a clot, what if it moves?'

Kieran reassured her. 'I'll give you blood-thinning drugs to slow any further clots forming, and we'll put that leg in elastic hose. Then we wait.'

Back at the station Kieran filled Sally in on what he required, before turning to Abby. 'You were on to the idea of DVT straight away, weren't you? That's why you asked about those jeans.'

Abby shrugged. 'They're such an unusual style I didn't think they came from around here.'

'You were really good with Jane.' Another of those beguiling smiles lifted the corner of his mouth.

Trying to get back on side with her? Warmth trickled through her, banishing all traces of her earlier mood. If he could try, so could she. 'I do listen to everything a patient says, not just their comments about aches or pains.'

'You have an analytical mind when you're dealing with patients. Ever consider studying medicine? You'd be a brilliant doctor.'

Bam. The warmth evaporated. As quickly as it had come. She reached for the next patient file. 'It crossed my mind once, but nursing suits me better.' Glancing at the notes in her hand, she said, 'Looks like we've got a broken arm in cubicle one.'

Kieran stepped in front of her. 'Why?'

She deliberately squinted at the handwriting on the page. 'Looks like Mrs Webb fell down her back steps.'

'No, why nursing and not doctoring? And don't tell me it's because of the children. Olivia became your ward long after you'd finished your training.'

Abby looked around for Sally, for help. But Sally was on the phone. 'Mrs Webb's waiting.'

'You did look into it, didn't you?' Kieran asked softly. 'What changed your mind?'

'Okay, truth? I started med school but gave it up to come home to look after Mum when she got cancer.'

'You didn't think of going back?' His hand touched her arm briefly.

'I'd enrolled in the local school of nursing while Mum was sick.' She blinked away a tear. 'When she died I had one year left to qualify as a nurse. It didn't make sense not to complete that degree. I always thought I'd go back to med school but first I wanted a couple of years away from studying and to save a bit of money.'

And then Phillip happened. If she hadn't fallen in love with that scumbag she'd have been close to being a qualified doctor now. But he'd been her big mistake, and she'd lived with the consequences ever since. She'd also learned her lesson. Don't trust charming playboys. Ever.

'You'd have made a very good doctor.' Kieran's knuckle brushed her cheek so lightly it was as though she'd imagined it. 'You're also a very good mum.'

Stunned, she stared at him. She'd just spent most of the morning letting him know how angry and frustrated she felt about everything, and here he was building her up to feel better about herself. He was good, no doubt about it. Which only underlined how careful she had to be with him.

Sally hung up and turned to them. 'While I've got you both, most of the staff is going to the pub after work tonight. It's also a welcome for you, Kieran, if you can make it.'

'Sounds good.' Kieran flicked a question at Abby. 'You coming?'

'Count me out.'

'Why? You're a part of the team. You should be there. The evening isn't just about me. It's about colleagues relaxing together.'

She raised an eyebrow at him. 'There's the small matter of two children.'

'Get someone to sit with them for a couple of hours. It won't hurt them.'

'Sure.' She snapped her fingers. 'Just like that, get a babysitter in.' Her cheeks reddened. 'I'm a parent, Kieran. That means I go home at the end of my shift and give baths, make dinner, read stories. Children are a full-time job.'

'Believe it or not, I'm beginning to learn that.' He reached across and tapped the back of her hand with his finger. A lot of little touches this morning. What did they mean? Was he trying to get past her bad mood? 'I haven't been the best uncle in the world, but I'm working on it.'

She slowly withdrew her hand and shoved it deep into her pocket, away from the tingling generated by his touch. 'I know you need time.' But he was only talking about being an uncle, no mention of his role as a father. Her heart dropped, the tingling stopped. 'And Seamus? Are you working on what you're going to do about him?'

He met her gaze full on. No winsome smile now. Just a weary shrug. 'I'm getting there. In the meantime I'm trying to help you in ways that you haven't considered. Starting with tonight and drinks at the pub. Look how wound up you are this morning. A little bit of fun would be good for you.'

He was right. She couldn't remember the last time she'd gone out with her colleagues for an hour or two. It wasn't normal for a single girl of twenty-nine to be staying at home all the time. But until now that had never bothered her as much as it seemed to today.

She gave him a tired smile. 'Forget it. I have to go home at the end of my shift. You go and enjoy yourself. Everyone will make sure you have a wonderful time.'

CHAPTER SEVEN

ABBY still couldn't believe that Charlie was ensconced in the cottage, looking after the children. Charlie didn't do kids. Not hands on, getting smudged with mashed vegetables. Abby chuckled.

'What's funny?' Kieran slid another glass of wine in front of her and sat down beside her. Close beside her. Too close, yet not close enough.

'The thought of Charlie in her designer suit down on her knees, washing those two scallywags.'

Kieran's eyes glittered, fine crinkles bunching at their corners. 'Shame on you when she's helping out.'

Now, that was a surprise. 'What did you promise her? It must have been something big and expensive.'

'A little charm goes a long way.'

A knot formed in Abby's stomach. He had

truckloads of charm. Look where it had got her. The lilting voice that melted her bones. His warm smile filled with promise. She hadn't been able to resist him. If she wasn't careful, she might find she still couldn't.

'Thank you, whatever it cost.' She could get used to someone taking charge of her life. Someone like Kieran.

'Let's take these next door and have dinner.' Kieran tapped the side of his beer bottle to her glass. He referred to the restaurant attached to the pub.

'Charlie won't be able hold out that long.'

'Actually, she said to stay out as late as we liked. If you'd prefer it, we could drive down to the waterfront and choose a restaurant.'

'Next door is fine.' Sounded like they were on a date. But, of course, they weren't. Abby looked around at her work colleagues. All three of them. When had the others left?

'You want to know something? Charlie was ecstatic when I rang. She told me you never ask for help, that you're always doing things for her and Steph and never letting them do something in return. Why's that?'

Abby sipped her chardonnay, thinking about

the question. Was it true? Sometimes she did wish for help but surely the twins could see that for themselves and give her a hand without having to be asked? 'I guess it's a hangover from when Mum was sick and I looked after them. Dad was busy with the orchard so I kind of starting doing more and more around the house for everyone. It was always easier to do a job than argue with the twins about why they should do it.'

'It must've been horrible for you all.' His shoulder rubbed up against hers as they strolled through to the restaurant. 'Then David and Morag's accident happened. Talk about your family taking the hits.'

'I miss them all so much.'

'Yeah.' The word rolled out over a long sigh. 'Me, too.'

Kieran took her hand and wrapped his fingers around it, giving her a sense of togetherness that she'd not known before. It felt good. Neither spoke until they were seated with menus in front of them, each lost in their own thoughts for a few minutes.

Then Abby said, 'It took a while to really grasp the fact that David and Morag were never coming home again.' She swallowed hard. It still hurt. 'Despite the funeral and having Olivia to raise, for a long time it had just felt like David had gone on another sojourn overseas and would one day turn up on the doorstep with a hug and a smile, saying, "How's things, sis?"'

As kids, David had looked out for her at school, then at university. Even when he'd moved to London to specialise, he'd kept in touch regularly, making sure she was okay. The menu shook in her hand. No one did that for her any more.

Kieran reached over and laid his hand over hers for a moment. The gesture made her feel closer to him. They had something in common apart from the children. Some of the hurt dissipated.

When his gaze met hers she saw he felt the same. He said, 'It's the same for me. Morag and I never had a lot of time together, with me being at boarding school.'

'Didn't Morag go away to school?'

'No, she stayed with our father, going to local schools. They were living in the States by the time she reached college level. I didn't see so much of Morag then. Her skiing took up so much of her time.'

'I never knew she skied.'

He withdrew his hand, reached for his beer. 'She was tipped to make the British Winter Olympics slalom team.' He stared out the window, obviously seeing something far removed from Nelson. 'There was an accident. In my flat. At a party my flatmates held. Someone spiked Morag's drink. She didn't usually have more than one, maybe two. But someone got to her. She tripped and fell down the flight of stairs leading to our front door.'

'The injuries meant the end of her skiing?'

'Yes. My fault.'

What? 'Kieran, no. How can you blame yourself?'

But he did. The truth shadowed his eyes. 'As my father said, I couldn't take care of an egg in a carton, let alone look out for my sister.'

'Wait a minute. You said your flatmates had a party. Were you there?'

'No. I'd swapped shifts in ED so one of the guys could go to the party. He'd done most of the organising so it seemed fair, and I really didn't mind. I didn't even know he'd invited Morag.'

'That would've changed your mind about attending?'

He swivelled around to look at her, his expression bleak. 'I doubt it. I thought Morag was capable of looking after herself. How wrong I was.'

Recognition of his pain, of the reason behind his vehemence about being unable to care for Olivia and Seamus crunched in Abby's mind. Finally she was beginning to understand. Finally in a roundabout way Kieran had let her know what drove him to be aloof from what remained of his family. How could a man like Kieran forgive himself? Especially when his father obviously laid the blame squarely at his feet.

'Kieran, you can't go on blaming yourself. There's only one person to blame and that's the horrible individual who spiked Morag's drink.'

'Tell that to my father.'

Their meals arrived then and Abby took time to savour her fish and let Kieran regain his composure. Then as he began eating she changed the subject. 'How are you finding working in Nelson?'

'Great. Everyone's friendly and helpful, and

well trained. Their goal is the same as mine, to help people. Yes, I am enjoying it.'

She smiled at him. 'You look surprised.'

'I hadn't really stopped to think about it.' He smiled at her. 'Too many other things going on outside work.'

'The children.' She put her fork down. 'Are you beginning to feel at ease with the concept of being a father?'

His eyes widened, and he took his time answering. Finally, 'I think I'm starting to accept it. I don't deny I got a shock when you called me Daddy on Friday night. And more than a shock when Seamus actually brought me that opener. Though I'm not convinced he understood you.'

'I agree, but with each time I say something like that he's going to learn who you are. And with each little thing you do for him he's going to understand what a daddy is.'

'Steady on. I'm still getting used to the idea.'

'Don't take too long.'

'Don't push me too hard.' Kieran shoved back in his chair, feeling cornered. 'I've only been here a week.'

In front of him he saw hesitancy in Abby's face then she seemed to shrug mentally, as though thinking, What the hell, and said to him, 'Then you've only got seven weeks left.'

He jumped in his seat. What? How dared she? Wasn't he doing his best? Abby obviously didn't think so. Less than two weeks since first learning about Seamus and he was taking too long? *How long did he need?* Which was Abby's point exactly.

'Easy for you to say,' he murmured.

'I wasn't born a mother or an aunt. I had to learn, as does every parent. Unfortunately kids don't come with a manual.'

He stared at this determined woman sitting opposite him. She was only trying to do the right thing for her children. If that meant harassing him, then harass him she would. She was courageous, and honest, and very warm and loving. How many other women did he know who'd give up their dreams to look after, first, her mother, and then someone else's child? Not one. Her revelation about quitting med school had stunned him, but it had also highlighted her decent, selfless nature.

He'd do well to follow her example.

Her knife and fork rattled on her plate. Her hands were shaking. Because of him? His reaction to her suggestion? Reaching for her hands, he squeezed gently, surprised to feel her trembling. 'You're right, there's not a lot of time. I'll work on speeding things up.'

Caution flicked through her eyes before she drew a breath and said quickly, 'Then you'll be coming to the staff Christmas barbeque next weekend. Everyone takes their partners and kids and we have a ball. Play cricket, swim, run three-legged races on the beach. I'm taking Seamus and Olivia.' She hesitated. 'And you.'

Gobsmacked at her spunk in light of his earlier irritation, he sat looking at her, thinking how marvellous she was. Then a laugh rolled up his throat. 'Oh, no, you're not. *I'll* take you and the kids.'

She grinned back. 'In that tiny sports car?'

'I'll change it for something more suitable.' She deserved that at least. But darn. He did enjoy driving around in that car. 'Now, let's look at the dessert menu. My sweet tooth will not be ignored.'

'I'll settle for coffee.'

'You don't want to share some cheesecake? Or brandy snaps?' Coffee be damned. He could see the longing in her eyes. So why not indulge?

It wasn't as though she had to worry about her figure. That was perfect. 'Cheesecake and brandy snaps,' he told the hovering waitress.

And when dessert came he made sure she ate some by holding a brandy snap to her delectable lips. Big mistake. Her lips parted to take the end of the treat. Her teeth bit through the crisp confection. Then, as if that wasn't enough, the tip of her tongue slid past her lips and licked a dollop cream from the snap. He couldn't take his eyes off her. His spoon shook. He might think he had everything in control when he was around Abby but his body was making a liar of him.

Abby reached for the rest of the brandy snap, taking it between her fingers, holding it as though it was a precious jewel. He couldn't take his eyes off her. He certainly couldn't swallow the piece of cheesecake clogging his dry mouth.

Abby's eyes were huge. Her expression startled. He saw her swallow. Waited for her to take another mouthful. Wished she wouldn't. His system couldn't take it. Willed her to. Sighed when she placed the snap on the plate.

The waitress appeared, placed Abby's coffee on the table. And gave Kieran time to gather his senses. What had happened there? Apart from his hormones going on the rampage?

He pushed the dessert aside and asked for the bill. The restaurant had got too hot and stuffy. He needed fresh air, and lots of it. But it was just as uncomfortable outside. Had they heated up the universe? Without thinking, he reached for her hand and felt a zing of current between them. She moved closer, her sweet honey scent teasing his nose, crashing into his senses.

'Abby…'

She turned to face him, her eyes opaque. Desire? She swayed closer. He caught her shoulders, steadied her. And then he kissed her. Her lips were soft. The scent of her teased his nose, racked up the tension that had begun inside the restaurant. And then he tasted her. His senses exploded.

Wrapping his arms around her, he hauled her in against him, trying to make her a part of him. And he kept kissing her. Like a dehydrated man drinking. Everything between them had boiled down to this moment. One heady kiss. A kiss that enmeshed her in his heart. A mind-blowing kiss that sent waves of desire rocketing through his body. A dangerous kiss.

Slowly they pulled apart. Abby stared up at him, swallowed. 'I've never been kissed like that before.'

Only one woman in the whole wide world had ever kissed him back like that. Abigail Brown.

'You look like you've been knocked down by a tornado,' Sally chirped when Abby arrived at work the next morning. 'A bad night with the kids or a great night with Kieran?'

Abby dropped her bag under the desk and rubbed her aching back. 'I slept on that lumpy old couch of mine. Charlie had snagged my bed and when she sleeps she spreads out like a starfish leaving no room for anyone else. How her previous boyfriend managed I don't know.'

She wouldn't mention that the lumps in the couch hadn't had as much to do with her restless night as images of Kieran feeding her that brandy snap. She got hot all over just thinking about it. If Sally knew, she'd never let it go.

'Here I'd been thinking you and Kieran were having a good time together. He's wearing similar shadows under his eyes.'

'Kieran's here already?' So much for arriving before him.

'Cubicle four. Robyn from the night shift is with him until one of the day shift shows up. That's you.'

'Sally, could you put Barbara with him today?' As well as those food images, shockwaves from last night's kiss were still rolling through her body.

'You know it doesn't work like that.'

'Why do I get to be his right-hand nurse all the time? Give someone else the experience for a change.' She glared at Sally. 'And stop playing matchmaker. It isn't going to work.' Unfortunately. Gulp.

Sally nudged her. 'Cubicle four. A five-year-old boy has been brought in by his neighbours after being found hiding in their laundry. He's badly bruised around the head and has suspected fractures to one arm and a finger.'

Abby shuddered. The poor little guy. 'Where are the parents?'

'Apparently the police were called out last night to a violent argument between them. The boy must've been overlooked or had already hidden, too terrified to come out. When the neighbour found him and took the boy home, no one answered his knocking.'

'How can parents be like that?' Her heart thumped her ribs as she thought of her two children; their trusting eyes, happy faces, soft cuddles. How could anyone want to destroy that?

'Someone from Social Welfare will be here any minute,' Sally told her.

'They should've been there before he got beaten.' Abby stuffed her fists in her pockets. Some people didn't deserve to be parents.

When she slid between the curtains of cubicle four, she had her anger under control. Kieran raised his head as she stepped up to the bed, and the compassion in his eyes for his young patient softened her heart. He'd never do this to his son. Wouldn't that knowledge make him feel more secure as a father?

'This is Joey.' Kieran nodded to the thin child curled up tightly on the bed.

Large brown eyes watched Abby warily as she moved to the bedside. No other part of him moved. Ugly purple bruises stained his arms and forehead. Abby wanted to lift him into her arms and cuddle him for ever.

'Hi, Joey. I'm Abby and I'm going to look after you now.' Those fearful eyes flicked to her face, but he kept quiet. The poor little guy looked exhausted.

'How old are you?' Abby tapped her finger on her lips and screwed up her nose. 'Let me guess. You look too clever to be three, but I could be wrong.'

Nothing.

'Just teasing. You're really four. Although you're quite big for four.'

Joey turned his head slowly to one side and back.

'Okay, I'm really dumb, aren't I? You're six.'

Again the head moved from side to side. Then Joey blinked. His mouth opened enough for him to whisper, 'I'm five.'

'Go on, you're not.'

'Am so.' The whisper was now a little stronger.

'A schoolboy. Wow. Cool bananas.'

'I like school.'

Kieran tapped her on the shoulder. 'We need to get Joey out of his clothes and into a hospital gown. Robyn's getting a warm blanket. I'm surprised he's not hypothermic.'

A middle-aged man spoke from the corner of the cubicle. 'When I found him he was curled up in the washing basket amongst the clean washing so he probably kept warm throughout the night.'

'Thank goodness he went to your place and didn't hide outside, or we could have a whole different scenario on our hands,' Kieran acknowledged, before nodding to Abby to follow him out where he spoke quietly. 'You're doing great with Joey. That's the most we've got from him so far. Can you stay with him while we sort out what's going to happen next?'

'Of course.' Try and keep her away. This child needed her.

'Joey's undersized for his age. Hopefully the paediatrician will admit him for a full assessment.'

'Then what? He'll go home to more of the same.' Abby couldn't help the despair breaking through her resolve to be totally professional with this case. How could she be? That gorgeous little boy was hurting, inside and out. He needed loving, not beating.

'Unfortunately we have to hand him over to the system.' Kieran's finger touched her cheek briefly, his eyes full of the same emotions she felt. 'In the meantime, let's make him as comfortable as possible and show him not everyone's a monster.' Digging into his pocket, he withdrew some money. 'I'm sure there's something in the cafeteria that little boys love to eat.'

'Definitely far more exciting things than what the main kitchen will come up with.'

'You want to go and get something before relieving Robyn?'

'On my way.' Abby snagged the note from his fingers and smiled at Kieran. 'You've got the right instincts when it comes to children. You know that?'

'Not a clue, but with you enlightening me all the time I'm sure I'll catch on eventually.'

Cheeky so-and-so. His smile warmed her to her toes, and she nearly whistled as she hurried to the café, all thoughts of Joey's situation momentarily on hold. Once again her mind returned to Kieran's kiss. A toe-tingling, spine-bending kiss that had blanked her mind and teased her body.

Idiot. She grinned to herself as she bagged a chocolate cake in the café. Idiot, idiot. She was supposed to be keeping Kieran at arm's length. But it was getting harder by the minute to ignore the effect he had on her. She felt more alive than she had in years. Perhaps she should just enjoy

Kieran, have some fun, and make the most of whatever happened between them. The problem with that brainwave would be how to get over him when he left again. But her grin stretched further. She couldn't even get over last night's kiss.

Dale Carlisle, Joey's mother, and the social worker arrived simultaneously, the mother causing pandemonium as she ranted and raved at the top of her voice about neighbours poking their noses where they shouldn't. Kieran offered his office to the social worker but Dale refused to accompany her, insisting on staying with her son, then verbally abusing Abby when she tried to take Joey to Radiology.

Kieran intervened, standing between Abby and Joey's mother. 'Dale, please don't talk to my staff like that. We're only looking after Joey.'

Abby appreciated the protection, although she didn't need it. Having Kieran stand up for her felt good.

Dale sagged into the chair beside Joey's bed and tipped her head back. The hood of her sweatshirt slid off her face, revealing bruises on her forehead and cheek. So Joey hadn't been the only one to take a beating last night.

Abby shivered. It was impossible for her to imagine living with a thug. She knew she wouldn't stand for it but, then, she hadn't been ground down by a lifetime of beatings and bullying.

Kieran tried again. 'Joey needs X-rays. Then he's going to have a cast put on that arm before being admitted to the paediatric ward for a few days.'

'You can't keep him here. His dad'll go ballistic. The kid's coming home with me.' Dale's eyes flicked left and right, left and right, her agitation growing. 'I want to take Joey home *now*. He's not seeing no social worker.'

The little boy curled up tighter than ever on the bed, one small hand clutching at Abby's uniform. Her heart squeezed for him. His gaze seemed fixed on a spot on the wall behind her, as though his mind had gone somewhere that didn't include anyone in this room.

Kieran remained calm in the face of the woman's tirade about hospitals and busybody social workers who didn't have lives of their own so had to interfere in everyone else's. But Abby could see his fingers tightening by his sides. He waited quietly until Dale stopped for air, and then said, 'Listen to me. Nurse Brown is taking Joey to Radiology now.'

Abby swallowed her angst at the young mother. After all, Dale was a victim, too. 'Dale, I'll stay with Joey until the X-rays are taken. He'll be fine with me, I promise.'

Dale muttered something under her breath as an orderly pushed the bed out of the cubicle, but she didn't prevent them going.

When Abby returned from Radiology she looked around for Kieran.

'He's taken a five-minute break,' Sally told her.

'That's not like him.' Abby wondered where he'd gone. He never left his post.

At least the department was quiet so he'd chosen a good time to disappear. Had the Joey incident affected him more than he'd let on? She wasn't going to find out standing here, so she'd make everyone a drink. 'Coffee, anyone?'

Stirring mugs of coffee, she was so absorbed in wondering about Kieran that she didn't hear him approaching until he said, 'Is one of those for me?'

The teaspoon rattled against a mug. 'Gees, you're doing that creeping thing again.' She turned, her breath catching in her throat. He was that close. If she just leaned forward a little, her lips would touch his. Like that. A soft touch. A loving kiss.

A loving kiss? She jerked away, turned back to the coffees. Reached for another mug to make one for Kieran. Anything to concentrate on other than the effect he had on her. Sugar spilled over the bench. She bit her lip. Hard.

Kieran reached for her hand, took the spoon and shovelled sugar into the mug while his other hand rested on her shoulder. If he couldn't feel her trembling then he had to be dead.

'I went down to the crèche,' he murmured. 'I needed to check on the children. Something inside me had to see them, touch them.'

Again she turned, only to find herself within the circle of his arms. 'Because of Joey.'

'I mightn't think I'm any good at parenting but I'd never, ever hit my son. Or my niece. Or anyone's child.'

She touched his lips, this time with her fore-finger. 'You're not telling me anything I didn't already know. But I'm glad you felt compelled to go see them. It shows you're thinking like a parent.'

Kieran's pager beeped before he had a chance to answer her. Disappointment warred with common sense. They were at work, and any moment now someone would come to see what had happened to the coffee. Abby sighed and picked up three of the mugs. 'Want to grab the others?'

'Sure. There's a call for me from Radiology. Probably about Joey.'

At the nurses' station, Abby pulled up a chair beside Kieran as he dialled the number on his pager.

'Two fractures in Joey's arm, but nothing else,' Kieran informed her when he'd hung up.

'Well, at least his head's okay.'

Time to change the subject. Abby said to Kieran, 'Did you bring togs with you from Dublin? Or do you have to go shopping before Saturday's barbeque?' She tamped down hard on the image of Kieran naked apart from swimming shorts.

'Togs?' His forehead creased in puzzlement.

'Swimming gear. Shorts.'

'Swimming? Me? I don't think so.'

'You can't go to the beach with children and not get in the water.' She grinned wickedly.

'Plenty of surf shops in town where you'll find something.' *Please don't buy skimpy Speedos.* Her tongue flicked across her bottom lip. There'd be no accounting for her reaction if he did.

Kieran grinned back at her. 'You've got a very expressive face.'

Then he headed toward a cubicle where an elderly lady was being admitted with chest pains, leaving her staring after him in amazement, her cheeks blazing. He couldn't have read her mind. She crossed her fingers.

At the curtain Kieran turned and winked at her. Obviously he had. Picking up their mugs, she went to rinse them, determined her face would have stopped glowing by the time she got back.

CHAPTER EIGHT

'UNCLE KIERAN, why's it called Rabbit Island?' Olivia bounced around his legs, her face and body liberally smothered in sunscreen lotion. Her cute yellow swimsuit accentuated her black hair and blue eyes. So like her mother. His eyes switched to Seamus. Again the dark hair and blue eyes. His heart lurched.

So like his dad.

'Uncle Kieran, are you listening?' She sounded just like her aunt.

He crouched down on his haunches. 'Yes, Princess, I am. Now, about this island that's not really an island. I'm sure it's called that because there are lots of rabbits here.'

Olivia spun around. 'I can't see them.'

'They're hiding in their burrows, away from little girls who'd want to pat them.'

'What's a burrow?'

'A rabbit's house. They dig holes in the ground to race down when there's danger about.'

Olivia's eyes widened. 'Show me.'

A sweet chuckle caught his attention, stirred his blood. Abby knelt on a blanket spread on the sand, plastering sunscreen on Seamus. 'You'll have to find one now.'

Dressed in cut-off denim shorts and a bright red singlet top that barely covered her midriff, her hair swinging in a short ponytail, she looked like a teenager. The compassionate face of the exceptional nurse he knew her for had been replaced by that of a carefree, happy mother. He felt a tug at his heartstrings. The sort of tug any attractive woman caused. Yeah, right. Abby wasn't just any woman. She was beautiful, on the inside and outside.

Abby appeared so confident in everything she did, but he had seen that flicker of discomfort when he'd suggested dessert the other night. Did she believe she had to watch her weight? When her figure was superb? It didn't make sense. Someone had to have made her think like that. Someone who had hurt her. Why would anyone want to hurt Abby? His teeth clenched. He'd like a moment with that person.

'Ah, hello, Kieran?' The woman in his mind

waved at him. 'We're looking for a burrow, remember?'

'Shouldn't be too hard to find one close by. I've got reinforcements if I need them.' He waved a hand at the staff members and their families sprawled over this area of the park, resting after an energetic game of cricket followed by an enormous barbeque lunch. He shook his head at how easily Abby distracted him.

Seamus pushed Abby's hand away and struggled to his feet. With arms outstretched, he stumbled towards Kieran. 'Raabb.' His foot tripped over a stick and he plonked down on his bottom. 'Raabb.' He put his hands down to push himself back on his feet.

A piercing shriek filled the air. Kieran jumped. 'Seamus?' He reached for the boy, caught him up just as Abby got there. Immediately Kieran handed Seamus to her, but she shook her head.

'Hold him still while I check him over.'

'Abby.' Panic rose in his throat. What had happened? One moment Seamus was fine, the next screaming his lungs out. Why? 'I'm the doctor. You're his mother. Take him and I'll look him over.' How was he supposed to sooth a screaming little boy? How did he calm his son? 'Abby, take him.'

'You're doing fine. Just hold on.' She gave him a tight smile.

Was that supposed to reassure him? 'Thanks a bunch.'

'I think he's had a bee sting.' Abby took one arm, carefully searched the skin, turned his hand over, checked his palm.

'A bee sting? Has he had one before? Is he allergic?' Anaphylactic shock could kill Seamus, he was so tiny. Kieran stared around at his colleagues and shouted, 'Have we got a first-aid kit with us?'

'I'll get it from my car.' Pete bounded away, a slightly bemused look on his face.

Kieran glared after him. Didn't the idiot understand what could go wrong here? Seamus tensed in his arms. Kieran dropped his gaze to his son. Seamus's face scrunched up as he sucked air for another scream. His eyes registered fury more than anything. His feet pushed hard into Kieran's abdomen, giving him leverage to stretch his body.

Kieran's heart thumped. His boy was hurting, and Abby wouldn't let him do anything about it.

'Abby,' he ground out. 'Hold Seamus. I'll look for the sting. He'll calm down a lot quicker with you holding him.' Seamus was never going to calm down for him.

By now a circle of staff had gathered around them, all offering helpful advice. How much advice did anyone need to find a bee sting? Pete returned with the kit.

'Found it. Hold him still,' Abby muttered.

Damn it, he was trying but who would've known how strong the little guy was?

Abby raised her head. 'There, the sting's out. All better, sweetheart.' And she plonked a kiss on Seamus's cheek. 'Now we'll put some cream on to take away the itch.'

I could do with one of those kisses. I deserve one, too. Kieran held Seamus out to her. 'I'll do that.'

But Abby took the tube of cream Pete handed her and quickly smeared the red spot on Seamus's hand with a good dollop. 'No need. All done.' And after another kiss on her son's cheek, she looked directly at Kieran. 'Just jiggle him up and down, give him a few kisses, and he'll be right in no time.'

'But I can't.' She'd turned away. 'Abby.'

Abby looked over her shoulder. 'Yeah, you can. You've been brilliant so far.' She lowered her voice so that no one else would hear her. 'For the record you just acted like a parent and not a doctor.' She winked at him. Then, damn it, she walked away.

He stared after her. A parent? Him? No, she'd got it wrong. He was a doctor. What was she doing to him? Seamus twisted in his arms and Kieran peered down at him. Soothing a child was definitely not his territory.

Seamus was hiccuping. Taking great gulps of air and building up to another shriek. Kieran felt a weird lurch in the region of his heart again. 'Hey, little man. Take it easy.'

Kieran jiggled his bundle as Abby had suggested, made soothing noises, and began walking around. 'Come on, my boy. We can do this. We'll show your mum we can put smiles back on our faces.'

Doing exactly what she'd intended. Kieran knew that. Knew he was jerking on the end of her string. But, hey, what else could he do? Charge after her and shove Seamus into her arms, crying and distressed? No way. He'd prove he could manage.

Just as she wanted. Cunning woman, he'd give her that. Then he stopped, looked down at his son gurgling and waving his hands around. *Hell. I've done it. Quieted the boy. Made him smile again.* Warm love, pure and simple, spread through Kieran and he sank to the ground, staring into the young eyes watching him. He glanced around and his eyes clashed with Abby's. Triumph glinted back at him.

Abby clapped and did a jig on the spot. She'd forced Kieran to look out for Seamus as a father, not as the doctor he automatically reverted to. And it had worked out perfectly. Another step towards being a parent achieved. The proud look on his face was worth the uncertainty she'd seen moments earlier, and which had had her wondering if she'd done the right thing. She had. End of story.

A deep laugh had Abby turning her head.

'I saw that, Miss Clever Clogs.' Kieran stood beside her, so close she could smell the soap on his skin, see the flecks of black in his blue eyes. His mouth was mere inches away. She yearned to lean closer to kiss those lips. What was it about Kieran's mouth that made her act out of character? Those lips sent heat flaring along her veins and scorched her heart. Her cheeks flamed. She scrambled backwards.

'Time for a swim.' Anything to cool off. She reached for Seamus and lifted him into her arms, using him as a barrier between her and the man now gazing at her solemnly.

'Let me carry Seamus down to the beach, give you a break.' The Irish lilt washed over her, like a cool, damp cloth on fevered skin.

'Guess I'm used to it.' She clung to Seamus, suddenly unable to let him go, needing a shield from Kieran's magnetism.

'At least let me help while I'm here.' His hands held Seamus's waist, pressing against her bare arms, making her quiver.

She definitely needed total immersion in the cool sea. Relinquishing her grip, she stepped away from Kieran's touch. 'Thanks. If I seem ungrateful it's because I'm not used to people wanting to do things for me. I guess I tend to take over and push people away.'

'No, people come to you because you're so willing to help out. That's how I see it. Others do, too. Who puts her hand up to stay late when a case overruns a shift? Who altered her sister's dress last weekend?'

Warmth slipped in under her ribs. 'But those things are part of my job, of belonging to my family. No big deal.'

Those were the things that mattered, the things that kept her grounded, helped her through the rare days she regretted having to give up her dream years ago. Anyway, what could be better than raising two of the most gorgeous children ever?

Someone to share her life with. Kieran. Shock tripped her. Kieran? As if. She might desire him, but love him? Her skin prickled, her heart slowed. This was the second time that thought had bounded into her brain. She couldn't afford love. Not with any man. She'd paid a huge price last time. Anyway, if she made the mistake of falling in love with Kieran, he'd never reciprocate the emotion. A cold weight of pain lodged in her stomach. She knelt down to place Olivia's water-wings on her arms as Kieran continued down to the water with Seamus.

Sally dropped onto the sand beside her. 'Kieran's spending a lot of time with the children.'

'He's just doing the uncle thing.' Would Sally never give up?

'But he's not Seamus's uncle, is he?' Sally watched, her eyes narrowed, as Kieran coaxed Seamus to step into the shallow water. 'You know, I've never noticed before how alike in colouring Olivia and Seamus are.'

Abby's stomach clenched and nausea soured her mouth. 'That often happens with cousins.'

Sally's eyes turned to her, and her hand found Abby's. 'I agree. But why does Seamus look so much like Kieran?'

Abby twisted away and stared out at the beckoning waters of Tasman Bay stretching for ever, at the smooth sand broken only by footprints.

'It's okay, your secret's safe with me,' Sally whispered. 'I'll stop trying to push you two together now I know about this. Though I still think he's ideal for you if you'd give him a chance.'

'He's a playboy, Sally. Playboys break hearts easier than I can break glass.' But it might already be too late for her. Somehow Kieran had managed to winkle in under her skin in a very short time. So she had to start acting sensibly, stop thinking about those electrifying kisses.

Kieran may be her son's father, but he could only be her friend. No matter what.

'He hasn't been behaving like one since he arrived and, believe me, there've been plenty of offers for a good time from the nurses.' Sally sighed. 'I heard talk last Saturday night he turned down two invitations to go clubbing. Hardly the act of a playboy.'

'Saturday night? He went to a party with Steph and her boyfriend.'

'According to Robyn, Kieran worked most of the weekend, including Saturday night.'

Heat pooled in Abby's stomach as relief poured through her. Kieran hadn't gone to the party after all. Her eyes feasted on him now as he shucked out of his outer clothes in preparation for a swim. Again the overwhelming urge to kiss him hit her, rising so quickly it rocked her to the core.

She needed a diversion before she acted on these dangerous impulses. She hauled her top off and popped the stud on her shorts, letting them drop to the sand where she stepped out of them. Across the beach Kieran stood staring at her, his face unreadable. But the flare of interest in his eyes as he took in her bikini-clad body was definitely unmistakable. He wanted her. Plain as day, Kieran wanted her.

And she wanted him just as much. Prefect timing, Abby. Absolutely brilliant. On a family beach with two children and most of her colleagues, and she wanted to make love to this man. Why hadn't she worn knee-length shorts and a baggy T-shirt?

'Race me, Abby,' Olivia yelled, inadvertently creating a much-needed diversion as she tore down the sand towards the water.

Abby raced after her, not to win the dare but to be on hand should Olivia trip and fall into the water. Olivia had had swimming lessons and now knew how to float on her back and dog-paddle in a fashion, and, most importantly, not to panic if her head went underwater. But she was still only three years old and Abby would never let her go into the water alone.

'I'm first.' Olivia giggled. 'Look, Uncle Kieran's undressed Seamus.'

'So he has.' She watched Seamus, as naked as the day he was born, and Kieran, thankfully dressed in beach shorts and not Speedos, make their way in a more dignified manner into the sea.

As Kieran stepped through the water, she watched the level creeping slowly up his firm calves, his muscular thighs, then… She swallowed. Turned away, focused on Olivia until she heard Seamus gurgling gleefully. Turning back, her face spilt into a smile. Seamus, held carefully by a squatting Kieran, was kicking the water into a frenzy while his tiny fists flew in all directions, putting Kieran's head in danger.

But what really grabbed her heart was seeing the look of amazement on Kieran's face. He was enjoying himself as much as his son.

Late afternoon the next day and the sun still blazed down fiercely. Kieran swallowed a glass of cold water. He enjoyed the heat, but couldn't get his head around the fact that Christmas was less than two weeks away. There should be snow covering the lawn, not roses and lilies flowering in the garden.

In her kitchen Abby had vegetables cooking for the children's dinner. Olivia sat on the floor, reading her doll a story from a picture book. Seamus had opened the pot cupboard and had begun removing everything he could lay his hands on. Kieran leaned against the bench, savouring the scene. Until now he'd believed domesticity to be highly overrated, had thought his married friends had gone gaga.

But what could be better than this? How could his parents not have given him the same sense of security that Abby gave these two? He thought his mother had but his memories of her were murky. Had his father not loved him enough to care how he felt? *Eejit. You know he didn't.* His breathing hitched in his chest. He hadn't been good enough to love. His father had always compared him to Morag, the golden girl. No argument there. Morag had been special, and he'd loved her. But why couldn't his father have loved him, too? Surely he hadn't been as bad as all that? The old bewilderment trudged through his brain, and he still didn't have an answer.

Dragging his hand through his hair, he shunted the unpleasant thoughts aside. No wonder Abby had been the nominated parent for Olivia. Abby knew what family was all about. But could he be a part of Seamus and Olivia's lives? In some capacity?

The thought of Seamus growing up believing his dad didn't love him appalled Kieran. He would do his utmost to make sure both children knew how he felt about them. These days, with emails, Skype and digital cameras, it wasn't difficult to stay in touch and keep a visual presence from afar.

Clattering pots brought him back to the present. He found Abby watching him, a doubtful smile hovering on her soft lips.

'You all right?' she asked.

'Couldn't be better.' His father may have let him down, but this family had begun to make up for his cold childhood. He felt as though he was coming out into the light after a long spell in the dark. Looking around, he drank in the simple things: food cooking, the radio playing in the background, the children. From somewhere deep inside he began to smile; a big, broad smile that he couldn't stop.

He moved to place a kiss on Abby's cheek. 'Thank you.'

Her finger touched her cheek. 'What for?'

'For being you.' For refusing to let him get away with his attempts to remain aloof. For making him face up to learning what he was capable of. Right now, he believed he actually could be a father. Maybe even a good one.

A thump on his shin stopped these thoughts. Looking down at Seamus pushing a pot lid along the floor, oblivious to obstacles, Kieran decided to join his son. Going down on his haunches, he picked up another lid and began 'driving' around the kitchen.

And around Abby's bare toes.

Toes with pink toenails. Toes that curled under when he blew on them. The owner of those toes tapped the side of his head. 'Remind me never to ride with you again. Your sense of direction is appalling.'

He looked up and grinned. 'Just following the leader.' A light air tripped over his skin as those hazel eyes peered down at him, a hint of humour sparkling at their corners.

'Typical. Blame the most inexperienced member of the team,' the focus of his attention quipped.

From his low crouching position her legs seemed to go on for ever. Something inside his chest squeezed. Excitement spun through him. It took all his willpower not to reach out and run his fingers over her smooth skin. Damn. He was supposed to be playing a game with his son, not ogling the kid's mother.

'Brrm, brrm.' Seamus pushed his lid into Kieran's leg. Focusing entirely on Seamus, he pretended to be unaware of Abby. At least, he tried really hard to ignore her. Impossible to do when his groin ached with need for her.

Thankfully the vegetables were soon ready. Kieran didn't know long he could've stayed on the small floor, ignoring Abby's legs.

'Do you want to feed Seamus?' Abby asked.

Absolutely, but he still wasn't overly convinced about the fun of mealtimes. They seemed highly overrated.

He must have shown some hesitancy because Abby laughed as she pushed the highchair forward. 'It's more about directing the spoon than anything else. Seamus loves feeding himself, which is why bathtime is after dinner.'

Olivia scrambled up to the table. 'I can feed myself. And I don't make a mess of my clothes.'

Abby placed plates of food and cutlery in front of the children. 'Don't rush your dinner this time, young lady. Remember what happened last night.'

'I got a sore tummy.'

As Kieran directed Seamus's sticky hand holding a laden spoon he chuckled to himself. Who would've believed a few weeks ago that he'd be feeding a small boy, really more like supervising the feeding of said boy, and enjoying himself. Certainly his mates back in Dublin would be shocked. Face it, *he* was shocked. Who'd have thought staying in for the evening could be more fun than hitting the nightclubs? Certainly not him. Until now.

'Going to share the joke?' Abby queried, one fair eyebrow lifted in his direction.

'I'm amazed at the amount of pleasure I'm getting out of this.'

Her lips curved upward, slightly apart so he saw her front top teeth. 'Yep, it's pretty wonderful all right.' Her hand touched his shoulder, her fingers pressing gently through his shirt.

Don't take your hand away, leave it there. He liked the warmth emanating from her. He liked the whole scenario. The kids playing. He and Abby looking after them. Then later, when the youngsters were tucked up in their respective beds, he and Abby would share a meal. If she invited him to stay on.

Suddenly that's what he really, really wanted.

To spend the rest of the evening here, with Abby and the children. But especially with Abby. Did that mean he should be running back to town as quickly as possible? Or should he relax and see how everything panned out?

'Where's the Christmas tree?' Olivia asked, bathtime forgotten.

They'd shopped for a tree earlier in the afternoon. 'Guess what we're doing next?' Abby grinned at Kieran. 'Want to bring the tree in while I find a bucket to stand it in? I also need to get the decorations out of the cupboard, too.'

'Olivia, come and help me.'

Abby watched Kieran take his niece's hand as they headed out to the four-wheel-drive vehicle Kieran had rented the previous week. Far more practical than the sports car but not half as exciting. Never had she seen him so relaxed with the kids.

Kieran seemed to be enjoying himself. No trace of aloofness showed. He hadn't minded sprawling across the not-so-clean floor to play mindless games with Seamus. Neither had he noticed the smear of mashed pumpkin and potato on his arm. Was he getting used to the children at last? Was he beginning to enjoy their company?

'Hey, where's the bucket, daydreamer?' Kieran appeared in front of her.

'Where's the bucket, daydreamer?' Olivia parroted.

'Coming right up.' Abby ducked into the laundry for the bucket then found some large stones to weigh it down and prevent the tree tipping over.

It took nearly an hour to place all the decorations to Olivia's satisfaction. Seamus did his best to pull the crackers open and had to be regularly diverted.

'Great job, team. That's a fantastic-looking tree.' Abby leaned back to survey their efforts. 'You are joining us for Christmas Day, aren't you?' she asked Kieran.

'If that's an invitation, I accept.'

Abby turned to Olivia. 'Bathtime.'

Kieran straightened from picking up pine needles. 'How about I zip into town and pick up a bottle of wine and some food while you're cleaning up these two? I'll prepare dinner.'

'Really?' The question sounded too loud in the tiny lounge, but Kieran had surprised her.

'Yeah, really.' His smile was slow and deliberate, causing a catch in her breathing. She loved that smile. So warm and honest, and sexy. Sexy? Had she said that? Not out loud, thank goodness. But definitely sexy. Kieran Flynn had always been one well put-together package.

Kieran waved a hand in front of her face. 'Hello? Are you going to take me up on my offer? It won't take me long to drive to the nearest supermarket. There's a mall at Richmond, right? I'm more than an able cook. Or would you like me to do something else first?'

So he intended staying here for the evening. Then she'd make the most of having him around. Maybe even get a bit further ahead with integrating him into the children's lives. 'How're your bathing skills?'

'I'm very capable of taking a bath, though I do prefer a shower.' His smile widened into a grin.

Heat flushed her cheeks as an unbidden picture of a naked Kieran in the shower winged through her mind. Of course he'd be naked. How else did anyone have a shower? It had been hard enough, seeing him in his swimming shorts at the beach. That broad expanse of chest, those firm muscles that rippled every time he moved.

She swallowed. A flutter of excitement tripped across her skin.

'It sounds perfect.' Then it dawned on her what she'd said. 'I mean, the wine and dinner, not the…' Shower. Getting in deeper here. She drew air into her lungs. Held it, counted to ten, twenty. Felt Kieran standing beside her. Breathed out, and turned to look at him. And immediately wished she hadn't. Similar emotions reflected back at her from his eyes.

His finger lifted her chin up until their gazes caught, held. 'It does, doesn't it?'

His mouth came closer to hers, and closer, until slowly, tenderly his lips brushed over hers, came back and covered her mouth. The kiss was long and slow, and filled with promise, igniting the tiny flame of need that had mostly sat curled in the pit of her stomach since the day Kieran had arrived, so that now it flared through her body, making her tremble and reach her arms up and around him. To hold him, to feel his lean body against hers, to taste his mouth on hers. Bliss. She gave herself up to the moment, to Kieran, knowing full well this was as good as it was ever going to get.

'Abby, are you kissing Uncle Kieran?'

Olivia's high voice screeched across her senses, slamming her back into reality. Jerking away from Kieran, she stared down at her niece as though for the first time ever.

Kieran saved her from having to answer. 'No, Olivia, Uncle Kieran was kissing Abby.' Then he looked at her, his eyes the colour of the sky on a hot summer's day. 'Guess we'll have to finish this later. Which am I doing first? Bathing?' He grinned. 'Or shopping?'

Shaken by her overwhelming feelings, she shook her head at him. 'I put a bottle of Pinot Gris in the fridge this morning. I hoped you might stay for dinner.'

His eyebrows rose. 'You didn't say anything.'

'Just thought I'd see how the afternoon went.'

'So what am I cooking? I presume you've got that covered, too.' He ran the back of his finger down her cheek. 'You really are a very organised woman.'

Is that a bad thing? 'I have to be, what with balancing my job and the kids, not to mention Dad and the sisters.'

'Take it as a compliment, not a criticism.' Kieran crossed the kitchen to open the fridge. Reaching for the wine, he asked, 'Did you plan on having this chicken? Good. I'll make a Thai dish if you've the ingredients. But first let's have a drink and get these two rascals organised.'

Bathtime was always a hoot, with lots of water finding its way onto the floor as plastic ducks and boats made difficult manoeuvres around legs and bottoms. Getting clean was the least popular part of the whole operation for Seamus and Olivia, but Abby loved this time of the day.

'Looks like you should be back in your bikini,' Kieran quipped from where he leaned against the doorframe, his glass of wine in one hand.

She reached for the drink he'd placed on the window-sill for her, out of danger of being hit by a flying duck. 'Or my raincoat.'

If only this could last for ever. But she had to remember that Kieran would soon leave them to go back to his safe and secure way of life. He hadn't changed that much.

'I'll start cooking shortly. I thought you might like a few moments to sit quietly once these two are in bed.'

'Sounds heavenly.' And it did. She wasn't used to anyone else taking over and giving her a break, but Kieran did it so easily, so naturally, that she found it easy to accept.

Scary stuff. Could it be she was getting too comfortable with him? If so, she'd get a rude awakening when he left Nelson.

The scent of sweet chilli wafted through the cottage when she sat down at the table and Kieran placed the meal on the table. 'A proper grown-up meal.'

'You don't eat the same as you give the children?'

He looked so horrified she laughed. 'Not quite. I'm exaggerating about the adult food because there are the meals I have with Dad and the twins.' She looked up from salivating over her plate. 'But to have something spicy and different, here at home, this is what I miss. I love exotic foods and used to cook them all the time, hence the well-stocked pantry. I suspect some of those spices have lost their taste they're so old.'

'Most seemed fine to me.'

She relaxed, reached for her fork and took a mouthful of chicken. 'Delicious. Thank you for doing this.'

'If we're thanking each other, then thank you for a wonderful weekend.' He caught her gaze. 'I've enjoyed every minute of it. But I'm happy to admit that sitting down to share a quiet meal together without little voices demanding attention all the time has its benefits.'

'You don't mind tempting the gods, then?'

He frowned. 'The ones who keep little children sound asleep at night? Surely we won't hear another peep out of either of them now? They're exhausted.'

'Let's eat and enjoy while we can. Believe me, when it's quiet around here you make the most of it.'

Kieran looked thoughtful throughout dinner and his conversation was desultory. Abby wondered what was going on in his mind. When she looked up from taking her last mouthful his gaze on her was so intent she squirmed.

'What? Have I got sauce on my chin or grown a horn on my head?'

He shook his head, smiling. 'Nothing like that.'

'Then what?' She hated being stared at. When Kieran did it she created all sorts of weird ideas of what he was thinking about her and most of them were bad. 'Are you going to tell me I'm a rubbish mother? Or need a haircut? What?'

'You're beautiful.' His finger and thumb twirled his glass back and forwards, but his eyes never left her face. 'I still remember the time I saw you coming out from Immigration into the arrivals lounge in Dublin. You were so pale and distressed, tired from the travelling and your grief, but my mouth fell open at the sight of you.'

Abby gulped, took a mouthful of wine, the flavour of blackcurrant and something she couldn't identify crossing her tongue. *This* she had not expected. Men didn't usually tell her she was beautiful. 'How much wine have you had?'

'Less than you. I'm not making it up. Plus, why would I tell you to cut your hair? I miss it being as long as it was back then.'

Abby shook her head. Someone tell her she wasn't dreaming, that Kieran really was saying these things to her. 'Unfortunately, having hair down to my waist wasn't very practical with kids.'

'Do you ever think about that night we spent together?'

She blinked. Her stomach squeezed painfully tight. 'Oh, yes,' she whispered. Her fingers trembled. She desperately needed to take another mouthful of wine but doubted her ability to raise the glass to her mouth without spilling the golden liquid.

Kieran reached across the table, caught her

free hand between both his. His thumbs rubbed light circles on her wrist. 'So do I.'

'I tried to put it down to the situation we found ourselves in. You know, our grief, the funeral with those two caskets lined up side by side.' Her voice cracked. Were they really having this conversation?

'Go on.'

She swallowed. 'But I couldn't. I don't normally behave like that, jumping into bed with someone without getting to know them.' She rubbed a hand over her forehead. 'That sounds like I make a habit of sleeping with men once I do know them, and I don't.' Kieran had been the first man she'd even wanted to make love with since Phillip. Unfortunately, the night with Kieran had been far more memorable than any night she'd spent with her ex fiancé.

'I never thought you did.'

Kieran's steady gaze burned into her as though looking for something. What? Did he want something from her? Another night in bed? Her toes tingled, her heart tripped lightly. Yes, her body said. Yes, her brain screamed.

Reality said no.

She wanted him, badly, but what would happen

afterwards? They'd still have the same issues between them. He'd still go back to Dublin. She knew she'd be foolish to expect anything more than hot, hungry sex. But, boy, oh, boy, what could be so bad about that?

Despite her gut instinct to believe in and trust Kieran, she knew how abysmal her instincts were. They'd failed her big time in the past with the two people she should've been able to trust most. Absolutely nothing could make her believe she'd got it right this time. She had to be the world's lousiest judge of character.

Pushing away from the table, she broke contact, anything to avoid those eyes, and then she began clearing up the mess on the bench. 'You're not exactly a tidy cook, are you?'

Kieran's hand touched her shoulder. She jumped. She hadn't heard him move. His touch was soft, relaxed and sent her senses into orbit. She wanted him.

Don't go there. You'd be playing with danger.

She spun away, turned and leaned back against the bench. 'I think it's time you went home, Kieran. I'm tired and need to clear up.'

'Don't shut down on me, Abby. We both remember that night for all the right reasons. Is that so bad?'

Absolutely. It undermined her determination to remain uninvolved with him. The memories teased her, tempted her to break her vow never to let anyone near her heart again.

Too late, yelled her heart.

Then she'd just have to undo the damage before it got any worse.

She licked her dry lips. 'I'm being practical. I don't see any point in going over the past. It happened and I've never regretted a moment of it. Not even when I learned I was pregnant.' She faltered, caught a breath and continued. 'But I've moved on. I don't want to repeat that night.'

Liar, screamed her brain.

He took her face in his hands and looked into her eyes. He didn't say a word. When she returned that look the world stopped. No outside sounds invaded their space; even the soft evening breeze paused as though holding its breath.

Slowly, determinedly Kieran leaned forward, brushed his lips against her mouth. Then he kissed her. Gently. Tenderly. And she responded. Her lips parted. Welcomed his tongue, let him explore her mouth. She danced her tongue across his. Slow burning heat unfurled throughout her. Then his arms came up and around her, pulling her in against his muscular body. And the kiss became demanding. She replied in kind. Meeting heat with heat, tongue with tongue. Desire wound through her, touching her here, there, everywhere.

Kieran tipped his head back and looked down at her. 'Definitely better than the memories.'

'True.' Her heart thumped as though she'd run a marathon. Her lips hated the loss of contact. Memories were colourless, flavourless, in comparison.

All the more dangerous. Her head jerked back. This had to stop. Now. Before they did something she would regret.

How she could ever regret being with Kieran was another issue, not to be dealt with right this moment. Now she had to keep her feet firmly on the ground and act as though she was way more sensible than she really felt. Sliding away from Kieran, she crossed the small kitchen to put space between them.

Kieran's thoughtful eyes watched her carefully. 'So why stop?'

'There are a lot of things we need to clear up

between us. Following this through will only make those things even murkier.' Why did she want to leap back into his arms and kiss him senseless? One thing was for sure, she most definitely did not want to be hauling on the brakes.

But someone had to. She had to. Her heart was in jeopardy. So were the futures of her children if she let that heart take over the thinking around here.

'I'd have thought "things", as you put it, were getting hot, not murky.'

The intensity in those piercing eyes slashed through her arguments and floored her defences.

'Kieran, you're not taking me seriously.'

'Oh, I'm very serious.' He followed her across the kitchen, stopping directly behind her, turning her, taking her face between his hands. 'Very.'

His lips brushed hers, a slow burn marking her soul. Her eyelids fell closed. Air snagged in her lungs. Her hands crept up and around Kieran's neck.

Dimly aware of a cry, she tried to concentrate on its source. Had she made that noise when she'd responded to Kieran's kiss? Must have. There it was again.

'Hell.' Kieran lifted his beautiful head. 'Timing's everything.'

Bewildered, Abby looked around, blinking. Then realisation slammed into her. Embarrassment followed. So much for passion. The cry came from down the hall. Olivia was calling out for her.

Again Olivia had provided a much-needed distraction.

CHAPTER NINE

THE emergency department had been frantic over the week leading up to Christmas Day. Abby stretched back in her chair and didn't even try to stifle the yawn stretching her jaws.

'I love Christmas, but why do people have to go overboard with everything they do?' she grumbled to anyone who'd listen.

'It's the excitement.' Pete elbowed her arm affectionately. They'd got on a lot better since the work barbeque.

'Or the stress.' Kieran glowered at Pete.

'Plenty of that, I agree.' Abby sighed. Sometimes it almost seemed too much hassle for one day. Nah, who was she kidding? 'Christmas is fun. I love it.'

'Have you done all your shopping?' Pete asked.

'Right down to the last stocking filler for Seamus. If I think of anything else, it's too late. By the time we finish here tonight, I won't be going near any shops. It'll be bedlam down-town.'

'And here I was hoping I'd get a dream run when I go to town at lunchtime.' Kieran shrugged ruefully.

'You haven't done your shopping yet?' Pete looked astonished. 'Whoa, man, you'd better take a three-hour break. But, I suppose, you've only got one niece to buy for. Just hit the toy shop and you'll be right.' He grinned. 'They also have great plastic trucks that little boys go crazy over.'

'Thankfully I've already done that. I just need to pick up something on order,' Kieran commented.

Abby scrutinised Pete's face. Had he guessed who Seamus's father was? It wouldn't be that hard. Sally probably wasn't the only one to notice the likeness between her boy and Kieran last Saturday. Not to mention how much time Kieran spent with Seamus.

Pete kept his face blank, but his eyes were twinkling with knowledge. Oh, well, nothing to be done about it. Had Kieran realised? One look at him and she shrugged. If he had, it didn't seem to be bothering him. Now, there was a turn-around. He'd been adamant he didn't want anyone in the department knowing. She sat back in her chair. Did this mean he was accepting Seamus completely? It certainly looked that way. Her feet tapped the floor. Brilliant.

Pete asked, 'We doing any work today?'

Abby grabbed the top set of patient notes in the in-tray. 'Sure. Guess the coffee break's over. Your next patient.' She handed the notes to Kieran.

'The boss has spoken.' He smiled and read the patient details.

'Yep, and here's yours, Pete. Barbara can help you.' Abby stood up and stretched her back before following Kieran to cubicle four. She may be tired but she was enjoying being nurse in charge this week while Sally took leave. It was great experience and she knew she'd done a good job, made easier by working with people she knew well.

Kieran was talking to her. 'I've never been as aware of Christmas as I am this year. While your shops are not as heavily decorated as those back home, and there don't seem to be as many carol singers on the streets and the weather's weird, there's a buzz in the air.'

'Could be something to do with being involved with children.' Let's face it, Christmas must have been lonely, even boring, for him in the past with no little ones around.

'There's something in that.' He tapped her elbow. 'Tomorrow morning with the kids and their stockings from Santa should be fun.'

'You have no idea.' She grinned and slipped into the cubicle where an elderly woman waited. 'Good morning, Mrs Atkins. I'm Nurse Brown and this is Dr Flynn. I hear you've taken a tumble.'

Mrs Atkins had fallen at the shopping mall, sustaining a suspected fractured hip. 'Got knocked down by a boy on his skateboard, more like. I don't know why those people in the mall let skateboarders inside. It's downright danger-ous.'

'I have to agree with you.' Abby took Mrs Atkins's wrist and began counting her pulse.

'On a scale of one to ten, Mrs Atkins, can you tell me your pain level?' Kieran asked as he gently shifted the woman's skirt so he could examine her hip area.

'Eleven. Dratted children. Where are their mothers?'

'I'll give you some more painkiller shortly, Mrs Atkins. I see the paramedic gave you a shot of morphine before leaving the mall.'

'Yes, he did. Helped to get me on that stretcher thing. Am I going to be here long? I need to get home. I haven't finished my Christmas baking and the family depend on me for that. My daughter works long hours at the fish factory so I like to do my bit to help her out. She's got five children, you see, had them late, and there's not a lot of money to go round in that house, I can tell you.'

Abby gave her a sympathetic pat. 'I'm sorry but until we know exactly what you've done to your hip you won't be going anywhere except to Radiology. Can I ring your daughter at work and see if she can come in to keep you company for a while?'

'Oh, no, dear. She can't afford to take time off. She needs the money for Christmas holidays. I don't think the factory owners would pay her while she sat with me, do you?'

Abby thought they might. Most employers gave their staff leave in these circumstances. 'I'll see what I can find out.'

Kieran nodded at Mrs Atkins. 'Let's get your

X-ray done. The sooner we know the damage, the sooner you'll be able to make some plans for your family.'

'Thank you, my boy.' Mrs Atkins hesitated, then went on, 'You're thinking I've broken it. I don't suppose I'll be very mobile if you're right. I knew I should've stayed at home to bake the cake instead of racing out to beat the crowds.'

Kieran looked taken aback at being called 'my boy'.

Abby winked at him as they left the cubicle. 'She's got your number.'

'She's one tough cookie. I guess that family is what keeps her so active. Unfortunately that doesn't stop her bones aging and becoming fragile. She's not going to enjoy her Christmas as much as usual this year.'

Abby reached over the top of the nurses' station and lifted the phone to call for a porter to take Mrs Atkins for her X-ray. Before she'd pressed any numbers Kieran leaned close, his aftershave alerting her to his proximity. She sucked in a lungful of man scent, igniting that deep longing she carried all the time now. Why did he have to stand so close? Why didn't she move away?

His arm brushed hers, and she found herself

holding her breath. Why? It wasn't as though he would haul her into his arms and kiss her wildly in the middle of ED. Pity. She would give her sisters away for one of Kieran's kisses.

Nothing had happened since the evening they'd decorated the Christmas tree and that interrupted kiss. She should be grateful because it was becoming increasingly difficult to turn off her feelings for Kieran when he only had to touch her and she melted. Grateful be damned.

'Radiology department, Clive speaking.' When had she pressed the numbers for X-Ray?

Swallowing and stepping aside to put space between her and Kieran, Abby quickly arranged Mrs Atkins's visit, then hung up. 'Who's next?'

Looking up, she found Kieran watching her. 'You're flushed. Need to take another coffee break?'

A break from him, more likely. 'I don't think so. What time are you heading downtown?'

'As soon as there's a lull.'

'That could mean never. Go now while you can.'

He laughed. 'Worried I won't pick up your present?'

'Not at all. I just hope you're not taking the sports car because it's way too small for mine.'

'Cheeky woman. Don't you know some of the smallest things are the most expensive?'

'Are you saying size doesn't count?' She grinned. Then really flushed. Bright scarlet. Spinning away, she grabbed another patient file and dashed past the station, Kieran's laughter following her.

'More than cheeky,' he called after her. 'Interesting.'

Of course, it took for ever to drive home with the traffic banked up as far as she could see. It hadn't helped that she'd had to call into the berry gardens to collect the fruit she'd ordered and her father had forgotten to pick up. Christmas pavlova wasn't right without strawberries and raspberries piled on top.

Olivia and Seamus were irritable in the hot car. The air-conditioning didn't work anymore so she'd opened all the windows a crack, with dismal results.

'Finally,' she muttered as she turned into her road. 'We're nearly home, kids.'

'There's a truck at our place.' Olivia pointed across Abby's shoulder.

'The driver must be lost.' What other reason was there for a truck decorated in a local furniture outlet's logo to be parked at her open front gate?

'Can I ask him?' Then Olivia squealed, 'Uncle Kieran's there. And Grandpa.'

'So they are.' What's more, they were both helping some guy carry a large couch towards her front door. 'What's going on?' she wondered aloud as she lifted Seamus out of his car seat in front of her garage.

After putting down his end of the couch, Kieran came to draw Abby inside to her lounge. 'I hope you don't mind but I bought you a new lounge suite.'

Did she mind? No way. The lumps in the old one gave her bruises every time she sat on it. Shaking her head, she stared first at the navy-blue suite that matched her apricot walls perfectly, then at the man who'd bought this furniture. 'It's wonderful, but why? I mean, you didn't have to do that.'

'Oh, yes, I did. If I'm staying the night, I want to get some sleep, which I most certainly wouldn't on your couch. I'd probably never walk upright again. This one folds out into a fairly comfortable bed. I tried it in the shop.'

'If you're staying the night?' Had she misheard him? 'What do you mean?'

'It's Christmas. I thought it'd be fun being here in the morning when the kids open their stockings.' He hesitated, a flicker of doubt shadowing his denim eyes. 'Is that all right with you?'

Her mouth dried. Kieran staying the night? In her house? She'd never get any sleep thinking of him tucked up out here and her just down the hall. 'Sure, of course it is.' Could he see her uncertainty in her face, hear it in the wobble of her voice? Try harder. 'It's a lovely idea. I'm only sorry you had to provide your own bed.'

That heart-melting smile that never failed to tumble her emotions beamed down at her. 'I don't have to use this one.'

'Oh, yes, you do.' Where had her father got to? Had he overheard? A quick glance around. No one else with them. Phew.

Kieran flicked her lightly under the chin. 'I agree. It's not the time for us to be getting too close and personal, what with over-excited children in the house likely to wake up at any hour. More's the pity.'

Pity? Downright shame, her brain screamed. But in her heart she knew it was best. It couldn't happen. Kieran wasn't a stayer, and that was the only kind of man she'd be interested in. Something inside kicked her ribs, and she gasped. What? She was never going to be interested in any kind of man. Remember? But apparently she'd forgotten because it was far too late. She was very, very interested in Kieran Flynn. Somewhere between patients and kids he'd managed to wind a thread around her and draw her in. She was more than hooked. She was a goner.

Abby tripped in her haste to put some space between them, which only brought Kieran closer as he caught her elbow to steady her. She stared up at him, and felt tenderness steal across her tense muscles as she noted the black curls falling over his forehead, giving him a rakish look. Her fingers itched as she fought not to reach up and touch those gorgeous locks.

She pulled away and stumbled out to the car to get the berries and other bits and pieces she'd collected throughout the day. Her heart hammered into her lungs, her ribs. Of all the stupid things to do, she'd gone and fallen for the man now preparing to spend the whole night under her roof.

This particular Christmas Eve would be the longest in the history of Abby Brown.

'I thought you might like to see these.' Abby stood over Kieran as he sprawled across the new couch, watching a lightweight movie. The children were finally asleep. Olivia's excitement about Santa had been a big deterrent to going to bed.

Kieran sat up, aware of the hesitation in Abby's voice, the way her hand wasn't quite letting go of the package she held out to him. His heart sped up. 'Are these the letters and photos you intended sending me and never did?'

She nodded. 'I figure it's time you saw them.' Her shoulders lifted slightly. 'But if you're not interested, that's okay.'

Vulnerability sat over her like a heavy shawl. Had she opened herself up to him that much in these letters? 'Abby, are you sure you want me to read them?' He caught her hand, felt the tremors running through her.

'Yes.' She jerked her hand away, backed to the door. 'Yes, I do.' And she was gone.

Kieran sat back, staring at the manila envelope. Judging by the thickness Abby had written often, or were there mainly photos inside? Suddenly unable to hold off, he tore the envelope open and upended it. Photos and letters, notes even, tumbled out onto his thighs. A photo of Abby holding Seamus as he waved at the camera lay on top. Here was the beginning of Seamus's life. Here was a window into all the things he'd missed out on. Was he ready for this?

Now *his* fingers were shaking as he reached to the pile of photos. Slowly he made his way through them back to the day of Seamus's birth. His breath stopped. His heart expanded. An exhausted but jubilant Abby held a tiny blue-swathed bundle in her arms. She looked gorgeous. If only he'd been there to see that moment. To experience the joy at the arrival of their son.

He'd missed out on that. Whose fault was that? To be sure, he hadn't known about the pregnancy, but even if he had, would he have been there for Seamus's birth? He didn't have the answer.

Tentatively he reached for the first letter, addressed to him at his Dublin apartment. Did he want to know all the details about Seamus's first months? Did he need to know how Abby had felt during those weeks when she'd learned to look after her son? His finger tapped a rhythm on the letter. Reaching for his glass of lukewarm wine, he took a long swallow. Then opened the envelope.

Time passed. The sun set, dropping behind the trees, and Kieran flicked the light on before settling down to read the extraordinary letters all over again. Abby had bared her heart in each of them. He wondered if she realised how much she'd given away of herself as she'd described Seamus to him. Kieran laughed over the boy peeing across the room during a diaper change. He sympathised about the nights when colic had kept everyone awake. And he wiped his eyes when Abby described her panic when Seamus had stubbed his toe the first time and she'd believed he must've caught it on some rusty wire.

'I panicked about tetanus poisoning. A fine ED nurse I turned out to be, but it's so different when it's your child,' she had written.

That Kieran could believe. His own reactions to children in ED had changed since meeting

Seamus. He'd changed in other ways, too. He no longer blamed Abby for not telling him she was pregnant. It hurt to acknowledge he'd missed out on so much because of his own stubbornness, but it was the truth. By being so adamant about staying out of Olivia's life, he'd made it an impossible situation for Abby. Whether it had been guilt over Olivia, or a niggling sense of missing out on something indefinable, he thanked his lucky stars he'd chosen Nelson over Adelaide for these two months.

Movement in the doorway caused him to glance up. Abby stood watching him, uncertainty in her eyes. Instantly he was on his feet, going to her, taking her hands.

'Abby, I'm sorry I made it so hard for you to tell me.'

Her eyes widened. 'You are?'

'Absolutely. Under the circumstances I wouldn't have told me either. I can only blame myself for what I've missed out on.'

It was disconcerting, the way she studied him. Then her lips slowly spread into a smile. 'That's the best Christmas present I could have wished for.'

* * *

'Here, get that into you.' Abby handed Kieran a mug of coffee. She felt good this morning after a really good sleep. Kieran's apology had wiped away a lot of tension. 'It might make you feel less rough at such an early start.'

'Being tickled awake at five-forty in the morning is certainly a new experience. Why didn't we think of drugging these two last night?' He winked.

Despite his beleaguered expression Kieran looked totally at home. Olivia and Seamus were tucked one each side of him in the pullout bed. Bulging red velvet stockings were strewn over his feet. Abby's heart did a roll. If only this particular Christmas wouldn't be a one-off. If only they were a real family.

Kieran grinned up at her. 'I didn't have a clue what I was in for when I decided to camp here for the night. Is Christmas morning always like this?'

'Yes. Last year Seamus was too young to understand but Olivia and I certainly made up for him. We got excited about what Santa had brought her.'

'Can I open Santa's presents now?' Olivia

demanded. 'Uncle Kieran said we had to wait for you.'

'Of course you can.' Abby raised an eyebrow at Kieran. 'Just how did you manage to keep these two in check?'

'You don't want to know. Ouch.' Olivia's elbow connected with Kieran's midriff as she clambered over him to reach her stocking.

A loud knocking on the back door was quickly followed by her father calling out, 'I've come to join in the fun.'

'Do you think we could postpone the party...' Kieran raised two fingers on each hand to indicate brackets '...until I've got up from bed and into my jeans?'

'You'll have to be quick,' Abby laughed. Then her mouth dried.

Kieran had tossed the sheet back and was clambering out, carefully avoiding children and stockings. Dressed in boxers and a T-shirt, he was sight enough to make her temporarily forget all about Christmas. Wow. As his jeans slid up his thighs she knew she should look away but her eyes seemed to have lost the ability to rotate in their sockets.

'Merry Christmas, everyone.' Her father spoke from some distant planet.

'Granpa,' Olivia squealed, and charged him, Seamus toddling right behind her.

Thankful for the interruption, Abby finally managed to drag her recalcitrant eyes away from Kieran and go and hug her father. 'Merry Christmas to you, Dad.'

He squeezed her back before swinging Olivia up into his arms for a big hug.

Then Kieran was at Abby's side, slipping a soft kiss onto her cheek. 'Where's my Christmas hug, huh?' A second silky kiss brushed her now warm cheek. 'Happy Christmas, Abby.'

She turned her head. Big mistake. Her mouth brushed his. Mumbling some silly reply, she jerked away and dashed into the kitchen to make a coffee for her dad.

Fidgeting with the mug and teaspoon as she waited for the water to boil, she stared out into the orchard. The apricots were ripening fast now, their golden colour bright in the early morning light. Or did everything out there look brighter than normal? Yes, even the sky held a depth of blue she'd never noticed this early in the morning before. Had her eyesight changed overnight?

It was as though someone had gone around with a paintbrush making everything much more vibrant than usual.

'You going to stir the bottom out of that mug?' her father asked from behind her.

She jumped guiltily. 'Sorry, daydreaming.' And her eyes went in search of Kieran, who was folding away the sheets and turning his bed back into a couch.

'So I see,' her father murmured. 'About our Irishman, I presume.'

'Shh, Dad.' Abby jerked her head up. 'The man's got a good set of ears.'

'Relax, he's busy tidying himself up. Maybe for you.' Her father actually winked at her.

'Don't even begin to think like that,' she growled, and poured the water over the coffee granules.

'Why not? I like the idea.' Max put Olivia down and lifted Seamus up for his hug. 'I bet these two would, too.'

She shook her head at her crazy father. 'It's not going to happen.' And with a deliberate shrug she added softly, 'Let's get on with opening presents. I doubt Olivia can hold out much longer.'

While the adults sipped their hot drinks

Seamus and Olivia got busy. Seamus upended his stocking before delving into the treasure trove of treats and small toys, while Olivia removed and opened each present singly, checking it out before dipping in for another.

Abby focused her attention on them, trying not to watch Kieran as he took delight in the children's excitement. But she did chuckle when he said, 'I can't believe how much fun there is in something as ordinary as a colouring book.'

'I should've got you one.'

'You didn't? Damn, there go my plans for the morning.'

Max got down on his knees and reached under the decorated tree. 'It's about time the adults got something to unwrap.' Picking up a brightly wrapped parcel, he passed it to Seamus. 'Want to give that to Mum, little man?'

Apparently not, if the determined look on her son's face was anything to go by. In a very short while he'd got the hang of tearing wrapping paper off his parcels and this one would be no exception. Except Kieran gently helped him hand the present to Abby.

Abby leaned over and placed a kiss on Seamus's soft face. 'Thank you, sweetheart.'

And then she tore the paper off a book she'd been hoping to get.

For a while the cottage was filled with happy discoveries and cries of pleasure as everyone unwrapped gifts. Finally Abby handed Kieran a parcel. 'I hope you enjoy your first New Zealand Christmas, Kieran.' And she kissed his chin. First New Zealand Christmas? Did she think there'd be more? She certainly hoped so.

He chuckled at the dictionary of Kiwi slang. Then his face changed, became still when he turned over the photos of Seamus and Olivia in hand-carved wooden frames. She'd had the photos taken in the orchard by a professional photographer who specialised in children.

When he finally raised his head Abby thought she saw tears glinting in the corners of his eyes. 'They're beautiful.' Kieran leaned across and wrapped his arms around her. 'Thank you. I'll treasure these photos for ever.'

Abby slid out of his arms and stood up. 'Time to cook the pancakes.' Time to put a halt to the heat stealing through her.

'After you've opened this.'

She stared at the small package nestled in

Kieran's large hand. 'You already bought me a lounge suite.'

'No, that's for the house. This is for you.'

Her fingers shook as she tugged at the tiny gold-coloured silk bow. Why had he bought her something else? Say what he liked, the lounge suite was for her. As she lifted the lid of the jewellery box she felt barely able to contain herself. Just like the kids minutes earlier. Lying on red satin were the most beautiful pair of gold filigree earrings and a matching neck chain.

She gasped. 'They're stunning. So delicate. So intricate.' Too good for her. But already she was lifting one earring out and slipping it in place.

'Perfect.' Kieran sounded smug. 'I knew they'd suit you.'

Her eyebrows rose as she stared at him. He was so sure of himself at times it was hard to believe the same man could feel uncomfortable with the children. What a mix he was. An intriguing mix. Sudden emotion engulfed her, blocked her breathing. Pushing the second earring through her earlobe she muttered, 'I need a mirror,' and dashed to the bathroom before he could see her inexplicable tears.

Of course he followed her. 'Abby? What's wrong?'

Shaking her head, she dredged up a smile. 'Nothing, it's just that I'm not used to anything as beautiful as these.'

'Here, let me help you with the chain.' He lifted it from the box and placed it around her throat, his fingers caressing her skin.

The throat that could no longer swallow for all the emotion stuck there. Why had he done this? Didn't he know how difficult he made it for her to stay uninvolved with him? Because of a piece of jewellery? No, because he'd gone to the trouble to find her something so lovely.

'Th-thank you,' she stuttered, and stepped closer to the mirror to put space between them. 'For these, and for—. Oh, I don't know, just for everything.' A tear slid down her cheek.

'Hey…' His thumb traced the damp track. 'This is supposed to be a joyous occasion.'

'These are happy tears,' she tried to assure him. But she was the one who needed the reassurance. Whatever she needed, first she'd take a shower, put some decent clothes on. Then there were plenty of things that had to be done before everyone started arriving.

Kieran looked unconvinced, but at least he backed out of the tiny room when she flicked the shower tap on. 'I'll start on those pancakes,' he said.

'There's no need. I'll do them.'

One long stride and he was back before her. 'This is your day, too, and I'll help all I can.' Then he placed another of those soft, soul-clenching kisses on her cheek, before closing the door behind him on his way out.

Abby's fingers touched the spot his lips had caressed, and a silly smile lifted her lips. Like a child, she didn't want to wash her cheek. Catching a glimpse of her goofy smile in the mirror, she laughed. She would put on the new dress Steph had given her two days ago for Christmas. She hadn't been going to wear the gorgeous emerald sun frock that made her feel so feminine. It fitted too well, showed all the curves and bumps that she usually tried hard to hide. But right now she felt she could handle it. Today she wanted to look her best. A T-shirt didn't do Kieran's necklace and earrings justice. Her decision had nothing to do with Kieran. Nothing at all.

Yeah, right.

* * *

Kieran was whistling as he made his way into the A and E department two mornings later. He felt damned good, so wonderful, in fact, he'd even been for a run around the waterfront earlier. His first run in weeks.

'What are you on?' Barbara quipped as he dropped down onto a chair beside her.

'Not sure but whatever it is, it needs bottling.' He grinned at the nurse. The Brown family and the way they had accepted him as one of them had something to do with his mood. Abby had her role, too. Had her role? *Red alert, boyo. Abby is the cause of this happiness.*

Somehow, despite all his determination to the contrary, he'd let Abby in. Into his lungs. Into his head, his muscles. Into his heart. A soft sigh slid over his lips. Abby. He adored her.

Shouldn't he be panicking? Shouldn't he be leaping up and stomping on the idea that she'd won him over? What if these feelings for her developed further? That would mean breaking his lifelong vow never to get involved with a woman.

Yeah? So? Things change. People change. I've changed. Because of Abby.

Where was she anyway? Running late, as

usual? What the heck, they'd manage until she got here. She'd probably slept in, exhausted after Christmas and all the effort she'd put in to making it a wonderful day for everyone.

He reached for the patient notes. 'Who's first?'

As he read the file his heart sank. His fantastic mood wiped out in an instant.

'Sorry I'm late. The car wouldn't start.' Abby sounded breathless as she flew into the department, all smiles. 'How's everyone? Did you all have a great day?'

That car was a problem, Kieran thought fleetingly as he stood up. He'd do something about it soon. But right now there was another problem. 'Abby, come with me.'

'Sure. What have we got?' She fell into step beside him.

'Young Joey's back.' His jaw clenched. 'This time with a suspected dislocated collarbone.'

'What happened?' Kieran asked Joey's mother.

'He got swung around by his arm yesterday.'

'Yesterday? Why didn't you bring him in immediately?' If they'd been able to treat Joey's shoulder then, it would've been a simple matter of manoeuvring the joint into place. Now surgery was very likely.

'Had to wait until the booze made his dad fall asleep.'

Kieran felt the heat of anger as it gripped him. Anger at the thug who'd done this to his family. The man Joey should be able to trust to protect him. A picture of Seamus smiling as he tore open his Christmas presents blasted into Kieran's head. Never in this lifetime could he understand anyone doing something like this to their child.

Until now he'd always thought his loveless, sterile childhood had been horrible, but it had been a picnic compared to what this little boy suffered. It was time he got over feeling sorry for himself. At least those two little rascals he thought of as his would never suffer physical harm. Not with Abby for their mother. Or him for their father.

A light touch on his shoulder, a gentle nudge at his waist. He glanced around. Abby. Warning him to take it easy. Telling him she was right there with him, that she knew and understood his feelings. Warmth seeped into his muscles, began unravelling the knots. They were on the same side. She was so right. Joey needed his medical skills, not his rage.

CHAPTER TEN

'YOU look gorgeous.' Steph grinned at Abby's reflection in the mirror as she peered over her sister's shoulder. 'I'm really glad you borrowed a dress for tonight.'

'If I couldn't ask you for help with clothes, then who could I ask? You are the clotheshorse of the family.' Abby laughed nervously at her image. This dress wasn't quite what she'd had in mind. The traffic-light-red suited her, but… 'You really think wearing a figure-hugging sheath suits me? What about my bumpy bits?' She touched her stomach, stared at her breasts.

'Suit you? It was made for you. Where're those earrings Kieran gave you? They'll finish the look perfectly.'

There was that word again. Perfect. Kieran had said that on Christmas morning when she'd first worn the amazing jewellery. Perfect didn't usually mix with her. But maybe she had scrubbed up okay tonight. She twisted around, trying to stare at her bottom. 'You're sure I have to wear the G-string?'

'G-string or no knickers at all. Your choice.'

'Call that a choice?' A nervous laugh escaped her lips. Steph and Charlie had dragged her to a lingerie shop and bought her underwear to match the dress. 'Why the push-up bra? I'm starting to look like a woman on the make here.'

'Then mission accomplished.' At Abby's gasp, Steph waved her hands in the air. 'Live a little, sis, and stop being a mum for a night. It's New Year's Eve and you're going to a party with the extraordinarily good-looking Dr Flynn. You'll have his attention firmly on you all night.'

Did she want Kieran's undivided attention? Oh, yes. If he was the playboy, then for one night she'd be the toy. Then hopefully she'd have got him out of her system and could go back to being that mum, happy with her lot.

Abby ignored the knot of excitement that had been threatening to spring apart all afternoon at the thought of going on a real date with Kieran. Instead, she slipped the fine wire hooks through her earlobes and turned to hug her sister. 'Thanks so much. It's lovely to be wearing something that's not stained with kiddy food. I feel like a real person for a change.'

'You're a real person all the time. Don't you think we all appreciate you? Abby, your family loves you. But if a change of clothes makes you feel whole then I'm going to donate my wardrobe to you and start afresh for myself.'

'I don't go out enough to wear that many clothes.'

'I'll have you know I don't have as many as you're intimating.'

Abby merely rolled her eyes.

Steph laughed. 'Hey, don't knock it. I'm the sister with the same shape and size as you.' She tipped her head to one side and walked around Abby. 'Hair up or down?'

Abby tucked one hand under her ponytail and lifted it onto the top of her head. 'Up kind of looks elegant.'

'Down and loose looks sexy.'

Abby's stomach knotted. Sexy. Her? Not really. Did she want to look sexy for Kieran? What sort of question was that? Of course she did. Already Steph was undoing the cord holding her hair in place and splaying it across her shoulders. Seems

she didn't have a choice. And it *did* look…
um…sexy.

'I'd better wear it up.'

'Coward.' Steph grinned at her then after a
moment turned serious. 'Come on, you're keen
on the guy. Show him what you've got. Mind
you, he'd have to be made of plastic not to already have noticed. You are beautiful, sis.'

Words that Kieran unwittingly repeated when
he picked her up half an hour later. His low
whistle when she opened her front door to him
was involuntary. One look at Abby and his insides turned to mush, warming him through and
through. Sensational. Stunning. Desirable. But,
then, when hadn't she been?

But he couldn't stop staring. 'Abigail, you are
the most beautiful woman I've ever had the pleasure to take out.'

Abby's cheeks suddenly matched the colour
of her dress as she turned to lead him inside.
Her words tumbled out in a rush. 'Come in. The
children have gone across to Dad's but Steph's
hanging around to see you.'

Steph gave him a big bear hug and told him,
'Wow, don't you look a knockout, too.' There

was a wicked twinkle in her eye. What was she up to?

'Aren't you partying tonight?' He'd bought three shirts that morning because he hadn't been able to decide which matched his jacket best. A jacket he'd no doubt take off within minutes of arriving at Hamish Harrington's home since the outside temperature was in the high twenties. But he'd wanted to look good for tonight. For Abby.

'Of course I've got a party to go to. Two, actually. But I wanted to spend some time with Abby first. Sister bonding, and all that. I'm good for advice on some things.'

Abby took pity on him. 'Do you want a drink before we go? Or shall we get out of here?'

'We should get going,' he replied with relief. These sisters were an act, one he didn't always understand.

Driving back into the city and the Port Hills, where Hamish lived, Kieran had his hands firmly on the steering-wheel and his mind stuck on Abby. He'd known she was beautiful, even though she seemed to go to extraordinary lengths to hide it, but tonight she was something else. Sophisticated. Breathtaking. The deceptively simple dress highlighted her superb figure, accentuating curves, including the slight swell of her tummy where his son had grown.

His mouth dried. This lovely woman sitting beside him had him hooked. Face it. Inexplicably he'd always been attracted to her. But now she was reeling him in, centimetre by centimetre, stirring his blood, charging his heart, bringing him alive in a way he hadn't known before.

'Stop. You missed the turn.' Abby touched his forearm.

Heat sped through his veins. He braked too quickly. 'Hell,' he muttered, and slammed the vehicle into reverse gear, ignoring the perfectly styled eyebrows raised at him from the other side of the sports car. Thank goodness he'd kept this car when he'd gone back to the dealer to get a more practical vehicle. Tonight Abby deserved nothing less than a swanky car to go out in.

The massive home was easy to find with the numerous cars lining the narrow road and strains of music reaching their ears as they alighted from the car. Taking Abby's elbow, he followed the laughter and voices until he found their hosts, glad to get among other people and put some space between himself and the woman causing his brain to fry.

Introductions over, Kieran turned to Abby. 'Wait here while I get us something to drink.'

But Abby had other ideas and stuck with him as he headed to the bar.

'Are you all right?' she asked, a frown on her brow.

'Couldn't be better,' he told her. 'This should be a wonderful night. Everyone seems geared up to enjoy themselves.'

'No doubt there will be the usual number of headaches tomorrow morning.'

'Then I'm glad I'm not working.' He took the glasses being pushed towards them. 'Let's go party.'

Kieran's prediction was right. Everyone seemed set to have the best night of their lives. The only bad moment was when Hamish informed Abby that Michael's son was extremely ill with everything that could go wrong with a liver transplant.

The evening flew by and Kieran couldn't remember having so much fun in a long time. It rankled when he found he had to wait his turn to dance with Abby. 'You're a popular lady,' he commented when he finally had another turn with her on the floor.

'I don't think anyone recognises me as Nurse Brown.' She grinned. 'It's this dress that fascinates them all.'

He could understand that. 'If the dress means I miss out dancing as often as I want with my date, we might have to tear it off you.'

Her eyes boggled at him. 'Tear it off? I don't think so.' A flicker of doubt crossed those beautiful eyes. 'Not even you would want to dance with me then.'

Want to bet? Putting his fingers under one shoulder strap, he teased, 'Let's find out, shall we?'

She shivered, and he relented. 'Spoilsport. Want a cold drink? Out on the deck? It's stifling in here.'

'Good idea.' She tucked her hand over his arm and strolled outside with him, where they scooped up two flutes of bubbly.

At the edge of the decking Abby leaned over the heavy glass siding to gaze out across the harbour lights. 'Isn't this view amazing? I wonder if Hamish ever gets used to it, takes it for granted.'

Kieran watched Abby, not the view she was

referring to. 'I don't think I'd ever take it for granted.'

Abby leaned further over the edge and Kieran slipped his arm around her shoulders. 'Don't want you toppling over.'

It was an excuse to touch her. Dancing together hadn't been enough, especially as most of that so far had been more about shaking and moving and less about holding and touching. He could only hope that before the night was out the band would play some slower tunes and he'd have a reason to hold Abby in his arms.

'As if,' she retorted, but thankfully didn't pull away.

The music stopped.

'Time to fill up your glasses, everyone. Five minutes to midnight.' Hamish spoke above the babble.

'Five minutes to a new year,' Kieran spoke softly. 'What are you hoping for, Abby?' He knew what he wanted. To make love with this woman, to hold her body against his and stroke her skin, to inflame her desire until she begged him for release.

Abby turned and leaned back against the

siding. Her eyes were unfathomable. Were her thoughts aligned with his?

She said, 'More of the same, really. The kids to be happy and healthy, maybe a promotion at work, Dad to be okay, and the twins to get what they want.'

So much for being on the same wavelength. 'That's it? What about you? Don't you have a big dream in there?' He tapped her forehead. 'Something just for you?'

'Kieran, I'm a mother. Dreams are on hold. And, truly, I'm happy with that.'

So why did sadness lurk in those hazel orbs? He stared at her, trying to look beyond what she was showing him. 'I'm not buying it.'

'One minute to twelve,' someone called out, and Abby straightened up, looked across to where everyone was gathering.

She took his free hand and tugged him along. 'Come on. Countdown time.'

He went with her, joined in counting down to midnight, and raised his glass in a general toast, before turning to Abby and twining his arm around hers. 'Happy new year to you, the wonderful mother of my son, and a beautiful woman I hold very close to my heart.'

Saying that out loud made it more real. Suddenly a chill settled over him. In four weeks he'd be heading home. Standing on this deck in the summer warmth, surrounded by friendly, caring people, holding Abby's hand, the thought of returning to Dublin felt incredibly bleak.

'Happy new year to you, Kieran. I hope this year brings you everything you want.' She seemed to be looking for something as she watched him over the rim of her glass. She obviously didn't find it because her shoulders rose in a slight shrug before she tipped her head back and drained her glass.

'More bubbles?' He reached for her glass.

'No, thanks. I've probably overdone it already. Let's have our first dance of the year.' And once again she was heading for the dancing, still holding his hand.

Somehow he'd let her down. Damn it, he'd let himself down in some odd way that he couldn't quite put his finger on. But if she wanted to dance with him then he was more than happy to oblige. Hadn't he spent half the evening waiting for his chance to dance with her? Only to have her claimed by some other hot-blooded male before he'd had enough time with her?

And now, as he took her into his arms for a slow dance, he wanted her instantly, all of her. Again. Still. Abby felt right in his gentle hold. He drew her closer. Dropped his chin on top of her head. The familiar, sweet Abby scent teased him, embraced him. Stirred him.

Her feet followed his in time to the music. Her body moulded into his. Her breath on his shirt warmed him. Her hand fitted perfectly in his, while her thumb caressed the back of his hand. In the pit of his belly a fire burned. The flames licked his soul, scorched his self-control.

Kieran's hand squeezed her fingers so hard she missed a beat, tripped over his shoe. Slowly she lifted her head, tilted back in his arms, and looked up into smoky eyes that appeared ready to devour her. Against her stomach she felt his response to her. Instantly her body reacted in reply. She wanted him. No questions asked. No complicated conversations. Abby wanted Kieran. And the sooner the better.

Something flickered in his eyes. Recognition of her desire. Longing. A question. She nodded once. When he gripped her hand tighter she didn't hesitate but led him away to the sports car. Totally out of character, so wanton, she leaned into him, sought his lips. He kissed her back, hard and fast, and then they were in the cramped car, speeding down the narrow, winding road. Her fingers tapped impatiently on his thigh. Blood pounded in her head. Desire spread out, licking through her body like flames.

Darkened houses blurred past. The night air cooled her fiery skin. Within moments Kieran had parked in his apartment garage. He had her out of the car and into his arms in less time than it took to say 'Happy new year'.

They had to wait for the elevator, precious minutes they filled with hot, hasty kisses. Not those long, bone-melting kisses she'd come to expect from him but kisses that wound her stomach muscles tighter with each quick search by his tongue. Kisses that caught the corners of her mouth, teased at all her senses, drove her so close to the brink that she thought it would all be over before she'd even started.

'Kieran, wait a...' She forgot the rest as his hands spread down her back, cupped her bottom while his fingers did incredibly sexy things over her skin.

'You were saying?' he teased as his mouth

trailed down her neck, making her gasp with need.

'I don't know.' Her hands tugged at the buttons of his shirt. Her tongue tripped over his chest. Under her mouth she felt his shudders, and smiled.

A door crashed against a wall. Abby jerked her head up, stared around. 'Where—?'

'My apartment.'

How had she missed the elevator ride?

Kieran scooped her up hard against his chest and stepped inside, using his hip to close the door behind him, while his mouth claimed hers once more. Pushing her tongue past his lips, she tasted him and imploded at the heat there. Her hands snagged his shirt, hauled it up and over his head, barely breaking their kiss. Pressing her aching breasts against his chest wasn't enough. She needed skin to skin. With one quick movement her dress flew over her head and landed somewhere across the hall. Kieran unhooked her bra and she shucked it off, tossed it away. His hands cupped her breasts, his thumbs circled her nipples, took her breath away.

Then they were kissing again; mind-frying, nerve-jangling, combusting kisses that acted like oxygen to flames. Her stomach ached with longing. Her legs trembled with need. Her shaking hands tracked over Kieran's chest, his belly, circling, stroking, feeling him. Kieran. She wanted him inside her. Nothing else would do.

She wasn't sure which of them fumbled with the buckle of his belt, jerked the zip down. His trousers bundled at his ankles. Quickly stepping out of them, Kieran kicked them aside. Then his hands were on her waist and her legs were wound around his and, yes, at last, she was sliding down, taking him into her, feeling that wonderful moment when her body no longer seemed real. When all reality disappeared in a haze of desire and sensations that tripped her pulse and took her into another world. And Kieran came with her.

Abby stretched out her legs into the sunlight filtering in through the blinds that neither of them had thought to close during the night. She smiled at the gentle aches in her muscles. All her muscles. Every last one of them. What a night. Rolling her head sideways, she focused on the man who'd spent hours giving her enough pleasure to last a lifetime. It still wasn't enough. Her smile stretched. Brazen hussy.

'God, woman, if you purr any louder the neighbours will be calling the noise patrol.'

She laughed out loud and kicked her feet in the air. 'Bit late for that, don't you think?'

Kieran's grin grew. 'You…um…we were a bit loud at times.'

'I bet you get some interesting looks when you leave the apartment today.' Her stomach rumbled, loudly. Her eyes met his, and they burst out laughing.

'There's just no keeping you quiet, is there?'

'Try feeding me. That should work.' She sat up and swung her legs over the side of the football-field-sized bed. 'Food. That's exactly what I need right now. I'm starving.'

'Must be all that exercise during the night.' Kieran followed her off her side of the bed, no doubt thinking it was quicker than moving back across to his side. 'Let's hit the shower then go over the road to a café for a cooked breakfast. I fancy bacon and eggs.'

'And hash browns, tomatoes, mushrooms, sausages.'

'That hungry, eh?'

'Did I mention toast?' She dug through her tiny handbag for her phone. 'I'd better check in with Dad.'

Kieran chuckled. 'You're how old? And you're checking in with Max?'

She slipped his shirt from the night before over her head. 'Think I'd better explain that I'll be a little while yet. He might be expecting me to pick up the kids.'

But her father seemed pleased she'd stayed out overnight.

'Don't go getting any ideas, Dad. We had a great time and neither of us wanted to drive home after the party.' She crossed her fingers at the little white fib.

'Sure thing, love.' Was that an I-know-exactly-what-you've-been-up-to smile in his voice? Couldn't be. This was her father.

He was still talking and she struggled to concentrate. 'Everything's in hand here. I'm going to take the youngsters to the beach later. Steph and Andrew are coming with us. Why don't you two join us after your breakfast?'

'Sounds like a plan.' Steph and Andrew going to the beach with Dad and the kids? Those two seemed to be getting very domestic these days, and spending more time with the family. What was going on? Had she missed something? Could Steph be settling down?

After hanging up, Abby found the bathroom, where Kieran was already under the jets of hot water, soaping that wonderful body of his.

He watched with hungry eyes as she drew her shirt off. When she stepped into the shower, his hands caught her breasts. 'Beautiful.' His fingers kneaded the soft flesh. 'So beautiful.'

Their shower took a lot longer than normal, and mostly had nothing to do with getting clean.

'I can't finish this.' Abby pushed her plate to one side.

Kieran rolled his eyes at the one sausage left. 'A rugby prop wouldn't have done any better. I'll be surprised if you can get off your chair any time in the next hour.'

'A gentleman wouldn't say things like that.' She grinned, totally at ease with the huge meal she'd just devoured.

'Guess what?'

'Yeah, I know, you're not one.' Not quite true. Mr Playboy was very definitely a gentleman most of the time. She squirmed as memories of the party crept back. Kieran had been very attentive all evening, making sure she always had a drink when she'd wanted one, holding her supper plate for her. Yes, but playboys did that. It was part of their charisma to be so helpful. But he'd turned down all those offers to dance with just about every female at the party. He'd danced with Hamish's wife but it would've been bad manners not to dance with his hostess.

No, for all she'd seen, Kieran had wanted to spend the time with her. If anyone had been out of line, it had been her. She'd accepted every invitation to hit the dance floor that had come her way. How had he felt about that? Had she hurt him by not staying by his side all night? Time for damage control. 'Thank you for such a wonderful time last night, all of it. I can't think when I last partied so hard.'

'You don't go out much, do you?' Kieran watched her through hooded eyes, giving nothing away. 'Tell me why. Is it because of your ex-fiancé?'

Talk about grabbing her attention. 'That's old hat. You don't really want to know.' Why did he have to ask about the man who'd hurt her so badly? Today of all days.

'Yeah, I do. I want to know a whole heap of things about you. I'm really interested. So, why didn't you marry him?'

'Because I found out I wasn't the only female sharing his bed. Even my bridesmaid enjoyed his favours.'

Kieran wrapped her hand in his. 'That must have hurt terribly.'

'It did.' But it wasn't hurting half as much as usual. Had she finally begun to let it go? Because of Kieran? 'I didn't know a thing about his philandering until the day I caught him with my bridesmaid a week before the wedding. After that people at work were quick to tell me about all the other indiscretions.'

'He worked at the hospital?'

'Dr Phillip de Hendez, general surgeon.'

'*The* Dr de Hendez? The one who tarnished his reputation trying to cover up a mistake in the operating theatre by pushing the blame onto his house surgeon?'

'The very same one. I see the hospital gossip mill is still working on that one.' A touch of bitterness coloured her voice. She'd have hoped by now that anything to do with Phillip would've been forgotten.

'From what I hear, it did the hospital a lot of damage. He was the reason I was so rigorously checked out before I got the nod to come.' He still held her hand, and now he squeezed it gently. 'Looks like you're better off without him.'

Oh, yes, heaps better off. Phillip's ego had always needed stroking, bolstering. At the time she hadn't realised she wouldn't be good enough for him. 'You're right.'

He changed the subject again. 'You know something? I had a lot of fun last night, too.' Those all-seeing eyes held her gaze. 'From the moment I picked you up the night became special. I admit to being blinded by the sight of you in that dress. My driving may have been very erratic, for all I know.'

The dress she still wore. Who took extra clothing to a party? 'Yeah, you were a bit fast.' On all accounts. Right down to that morning's shower. And she'd been with him all the way.

Now she wanted more of what they'd shared last night. Not just today, but every day. She wanted Kieran in her life, full time. Like that was ever going to happen. In the end she'd only get hurt. And sooner rather than later as he would be heading home. She should be distancing herself from him, not getting involved. But it had been wonderful.

Glancing at her watch, she sighed. 'I probably should be getting home.'

'That's a shame.' But he stood up and held her chair for her. 'I'll have to talk to Steph and Charlie and make sure they look after the children more so you can have other fun.'

The sizzle under her skin began to fade. 'Kieran, I might have had a wonderful time with you but I don't want anyone else in my life at the moment. Neither do the kids.' Some time between the dancing and the sheets she'd fallen in love with him. Or had that happened long before, two years ago, and only now was she admitting it? Relief settled over her. She would never marry Kieran but at least she could admit to loving him. Sadness replaced her relief. Was she doomed to unrequited love? Yes, without doubt.

'Abby...' He hesitated then went on, 'I'm going back to Ireland soon.' Caution filled his eyes, quickly followed by guilt.

Did he really feel bad about leaving the children? She doubted his guilt had anything to do with her. 'I know that.'

He looked desperate for her to understand. 'Coming here has turned out to be the best decision I've made in a long time. I needed to get to know Olivia. She's my family and I've let her down badly.' He paused, struggling with something deep inside. She could see it in his eyes, in his stance.

'Go on,' she said quietly, knowing she wouldn't like what she heard but needing to get it out in the open.

'Then there's Seamus. He's awesome. I love him. And that's been a revelation. I will help out with him the same way I do with Olivia.'

'Financially.' The word was sour in her mouth.

'I hope you're not expecting me to stay on, to be closer to you and the children. I can't do that.'

Well, she might not understand why he'd want to walk away from his son, but she couldn't say she hadn't been warned. He'd always made it absolutely clear where he stood on the subject of families. His Christmas Eve apology for making it so hard for her hadn't changed his stance.

'Can't? Or won't?' Her stomach clenched uncomfortably. The wonderful morning had fallen off track. Their camaraderie of the last hours was being tested, and failing. She'd always known Kieran had no intention of staying and she shouldn't have expected anything different. But for a few hours she'd forgotten all that and had allowed herself to dream. What a fool she'd turned out to be.

Kieran was good for a one-night fling, maybe even a few more nights over the coming weeks, but there'd never be any more from him. He had warned her. Told her about his commitment phobia, explained why he didn't want or feel capable of being a full-time parent, let alone someone's husband.

The previous evening she'd thought she could do the one-night-stand thing, but she'd been fooling herself. No way could she walk away from what had happened between them and pretend her heart was intact. Not when she loved him.

Kieran said nothing as they walked back across the road to his apartment block garage. He pinged the lock on the four-wheel drive. Back to the practical vehicle. Her date was over. Abby suddenly felt stupid, shabby even. Dressed in last night's party dress, it was obvious for all to see that she hadn't been home. It hadn't mattered until now. Immediately she wanted to be at home, dressed in mother-of-two underwear, comfortable shorts and a baggy T. Cinderella back in the wardrobe.

Why had she fallen in love with Kieran? Another man who liked to have a good time but did not want to put down any roots? What was wrong with her that she could only love men who couldn't love her back the way she wanted, needed, to be loved?

CHAPTER ELEVEN

INSIDE the vehicle Kieran leaned his head back and sighed. 'I haven't made you any promises that I can't keep.'

'That's true.'

Two very bleak words he was responsible for. He needed to clear the air before the situation got worse. They'd had a wonderful time and he did not want that to be lost because of any misunderstanding.

'Abby, do you trust me to do the right thing by my son?'

Silence hung between them. Her hands fisted in her lap. Her eyes seemed glued to something beyond the vehicle.

Hurt stabbed him hard beneath his ribs. Why couldn't she trust him? He hadn't let her down since he'd come to Nelson. Had he? He couldn't prevent the hurt ringing in his voice. 'You've answered without a word.'

Her words came slowly, as though she was thinking her way through a minefield. 'I do believe you'll try. You'll probably stay in touch regularly, but that's not enough. The way I see it, you're doing to Seamus what your father did to you. Leaving him behind. You mightn't be cruel and undermine his attempts to do things, but he's not going to know you. You're not going to be there when he hurts, when he asks what the moon is made of, when he wants to learn to drive.'

'You don't pull any punches, do you?' he gasped, reeling from the intensity of her statement. Where had the soft woman who'd spent the night in his arms gone?

'I just want what's best for you all,' she whispered.

So they were on the same playing field. 'So do I.' He took a steadying breath. 'What happens when I hurt Seamus? How do you explain to him that his father had to go away because he failed to be a good daddy?'

She'd seek him out and throttle him, that's what she'd do.

'I haven't got a clue. I can't even get it through to you that you're already a good father. Like me, you have to learn as you go along. Why won't you see that?' She saw everything in black and white.

'Abby, sweetheart, you're a novice when it comes to this. My father worked at it for most of my life to get me to see things his way. Like water dripping on rock, eventually the rock wears away. Take a young child and keep telling him he's useless and he begins to believe that. Take that child as a young man and blame him for everything that goes wrong in their family and it becomes real.'

She turned, and the sympathy he saw in those emerald eyes nearly drowned him. But he didn't want sympathy, he wanted understanding. He needed her to accept he knew what he was doing.

But, of course, she didn't. This was Abby, after all. The woman who believed in families and happy-ever-afters. Although he had to admit those hadn't come her way very often.

She said, 'That's the most terrible thing I've heard, but you're nothing like that. Already your son loves you, because of how you've treated him with care and love.'

A knife turned in his heart.

'Your niece loves you.' A tear rolled down her cheek.

There was more. He just knew it. Except he didn't know what that was.

And Abby wasn't saying.

Kieran stomped hard on the accelerator. If only he had the sports car in his hands. After dropping Abby off, he'd turned in the opposite direction from the city, taking the main highway south, further out into the countryside. He needed speed to shake the shock out of his system that had slammed him between the eyes.

He loved Abby.

He gripped the steering-wheel harder to stop the tremors racking his body.

How the hell had this happened?

He loved her and the despair he'd seen in her eyes rode with him all the way, mocking him. He'd never promised her anything he couldn't give. But now he had to deal with this new development.

New? Get real. He'd probably loved her since that night in Dublin. If he'd ever admit it. How could he have missed it? He jerked the vehicle around a sharp corner. He'd been blind to what had been right before his eyes because all his attention had been focused on the children.

Abby. The woman of his dreams. When he'd allowed himself to dream, that was. Which hadn't been often.

So what was he going to do? Absolutely nothing.

How could he? He was his father's son. Which meant?

He'd be a useless father. That was a given.

He'd be a worse husband.

Because? Commitment scared him senseless. He'd been committed to his dog and Beagles had got run over while he'd been walking him. What about his girlfriend who'd lost their baby? He'd loved her and yet he hadn't been there when she'd miscarried. He'd been committed to Morag, and she'd been drugged and injured while in his flat. It didn't matter that he hadn't been there, he'd trusted the guys he'd shared that flat with. He'd committed to showing his father he could be a success and never once had he heard that his father was proud of him.

So how could he offer himself to Abby?

No. His lifestyle of love them and leave them was safer for everyone involved.

But.

Last night he and Abby had made love. Last night had been about the two of them, about giving and receiving, sharing. He hadn't been able to get enough of her, generous soul that she was. Last night he'd have been happy if they'd flown to the moon to be alone. He had wanted nothing more than Abby. No one else.

Inspiration struck him. What if Abby and the children moved to Dublin? He could set them up in a house near his apartment. He could see them as often as he wanted without making that commitment he was so afraid of. Pleased with the idea, he relaxed as he drove up the Spooners Range for view back to the city.

It would be a win-win situation for them all.

In ED Abby tugged her gloves off and tossed them in the bin, then stripped the bloodstained sheets off the bed and pushed them into the laundry bag.

It had been an uncomfortable few days since the morning after New Year's Eve. She and Kieran had been dancing around one another. He didn't seem any more prepared to break the uneasy truce that had arisen between them than she was. Whenever he'd come out to see the kids she'd made sure to go over to her father's house so there could be no awkward conversations about the future. It bugged her that Kieran seemed relieved when she did that. She'd hoped he might come round to her way of thinking.

Anyway, she'd come to a decision. It scared her, a lot, every time she thought about it but if, and it was a huge if, it suited Kieran, she and the children would move to Dublin. Then Olivia and Seamus could be as close to Kieran as to her.

The fact she loved Kieran had nothing to do with this. *Yeah, right.* Somehow she would deal with that. Somehow. Some time. In the next million years she'd get over him.

Sally stopped her on the way back to the cubicle with clean linen. 'That young boy Joey is in cubicle one. His neighbour brought him and his mother in while you were with the forestry worker.'

Abby's heart squeezed. 'What's happened this time?'

'Dislocated shoulder again, plus a fractured wrist. We're waiting on the orthopaedic surgeon, but he's in Theatre at the moment.' Sally grimaced. 'That poor kid. When is his mother going to get out of the situation?'

'I guess it's not that easy when you're financially up against the wall and being terrorised by the person you rely on for support. I'll go and sit with them until we get busy.'

Joey was sleeping fitfully when she crept into his cubicle. She spoke softly to his mother. 'Hello, Dale. Is it okay if I check on Joey?'

Dale nodded. Abby took her time counting Joey's pulse, checking his pain medication levels and generally straightening out the blanket. Then she sat on the end of the bed and studied the woman before her. Dale was probably younger than Abby but the defeat in her eyes made her look ten years older. 'Joey's vitals are good. What about you? Have you got any injuries this time?'

'Nothing too bad. Just bruises.'

'I should look at them,' Abby said gently. 'If you'd like me to.'

'Nah, don't worry about me.'

'But I do. It's just as important to look after your health. For Joey's sake,' she nudged.

In the ensuing silence Abby could hear Kieran talking to Sally. As Abby was about to ask Dale if she'd like a coffee, Dale muttered, 'Last time we were here you talked to me.'

'Yes.' She'd mentioned several things, including Dale getting help for herself and Joey.

'Something about a refuge place where we could hide from my old man.'

Abby spoke quietly, afraid of scaring Dale off. 'The women's refuge. They'd protect you and Joey, and provide a room and food for as long as it takes to sort yourself out.'

'It's not about me. But I can't let him hit my boy no more. Don't suppose you know what it's like for us. You got any kids?'

Abby smiled. 'I've got a wee boy, and my niece lives with me, too.'

'Is the father good to his boy? Your boy?'

Kieran put down the radio handpiece. Ambulance Two was bringing in a sixty-one-year-old male, suspected broken femur, abrasions and possible concussion, query other head injuries. He had been unconscious but had come round in the last five minutes.

Nothing overly unusual with those details. But. Concern at what else he'd been told by the paramedic clawed at him. With a heavy tread he headed around the station. Life had a way of throwing up wild cards when you least expected them. Outside cubicle one he hesitated, and overheard Joey's mother ask, 'Is the father good to his boy? Your boy?'

Abby answered, 'He's wonderful. Seems to instinctively know how to look out for Seamus. I couldn't ask for a better father for my son.'

Kieran's heart slowed as his chest took a hit. That was him she was talking about. Saying he was a good father. Better than that even. Warmth slipped under his guard, gave him a sense of belonging, of doing right. Maybe he was parent material after all. Who would know better than Abby? Hadn't she told him the same a week ago? Yeah, and hadn't he thrown it back at her, refusing to believe her? Too busy protecting himself to see how he'd hurt Abby? She'd been hurt enough in her life, he should be looking out for her.

Dale was saying, 'Lucky little boy. Joey's father can't stand him being around.'

Abby's sigh was audible to Kieran. 'Seamus is lucky. His dad loves him very much.'

Talk about a morale boost. Kieran sucked in the praise. Then thought about what he'd been on his way to do when he'd stopped outside the cubicle and the warmth under his skin evaporated. He lifted his chin. Now was his chance to put some things right between them. He'd be there for Abby, would support her over the coming weeks, help her out with anything that needed doing.

He stepped around the curtain. 'Abby, can you come with me?' Kieran took her elbow and led her out of the cubicle, not giving her time to refuse.

'This had better be good.' That aloof tone she'd adopted with him all week hardened. 'I'm finally getting somewhere with Dale. She's talking about the women's refuge.' Abby tried to pull her arm away but he tightened his hold.

'Barbara will see to Joey. I need to talk to you.'

Abby turned to him. He saw apprehension slither through her eyes. 'Kieran? What's going on?'

He led her to a chair before squatting in front of her and wrapping his hands around hers.

Which made her tremble. 'Tell me.'

'Abby, there's been an accident.'

Slam-dunk. Her face paled. 'Seamus? Olivia? I

saw them both at lunchtime and they were okay. What's happened?' Her mouth closed over any more questions.

'The children are fine.' Kieran's thumbs rubbed the backs of her hands. 'Abby, Max fell off a ladder in the orchard. The paramedics are bringing him in now.'

'Dad? Fell off a ladder? Why was he up one in the first place? He's got workers to do that.' She leapt up, spun round, fear written all over her face. 'He's going to be all right? Isn't he?'

Kieran quickly outlined the scant details he'd received from the ambulance crew. 'They've put a neck brace on him but they don't believe he has sustained spinal injures. It's a precaution.'

'I know they do that.' Abby blinked at him as though he held a powerful set of headlights directed at her.

Sure, she knew, but this was her father and when she first saw him there was every chance all her training would go out the window.

'How long before Dad gets here?' Another blink.

'Any minute now. Sally will let us know.' Kieran reached for her and held her against him.

He could feel her shock in her tense body, in her short, fast breaths against his chest. His hand stroked her back, trying to give her some love.

She pulled back in his arms. 'What else? Have you told me everything?' This was Abby the daughter, not Abby the nurse asking.

'When Max was found him he was slipping in and out of consciousness so we have to assume he hit his head as well.' Kieran kept rubbing her back in circular movements.

Speaking against his chest, 'I need to wait in the ambulance bay.'

'Of course. But you won't be there as a nurse. Sally and the others will do that.'

Sally tapped him on the shoulder. 'They're pulling into the bay now.' Then she reached for Abby's hands, kissed her on the forehead. 'Hang in there, Abby. We'll do everything we can for Max.'

'I know but what if it's not enough?' Her fear made her voice tremble. Kieran had to swallow hard on the lump blocking his throat. Not only was he worried about Max, but this caring, loving woman was hurting badly, and he couldn't prevent that. He *could* look after her father to the absolute best of his ability. Would it be enough? It absolutely had to be.

Abby thought her ribs would break under the thumping they were getting from her heart. Dad. What had he been doing up a ladder? He should know better. He was sixty-one, for goodness' sake. But he'd been up them all his life. Why shouldn't he use ladders now? How else could he check the fruit? God, she wanted to strangle him. Hadn't they had enough horrors in this family?

Family. Her sisters. They needed to be told. Something to do to fill in this fearful hiatus that waiting inflicted. 'I need to call Steph and Charlie. They should be here.'

Sally gave her a quick hug. 'I called Steph a moment ago. She's heading straight in with Charlie.'

Abby felt her shoulders sag. Now what? She couldn't stand still. But as the ambulance backed into the bay Kieran held her back while the paramedics gently rolled out the stretcher. Abby's chest ached. Her eyes stung. Her legs wobbled. And Kieran held her upright.

Get a grip. She was a nurse. She dealt with this

all the time. 'Dad,' she choked as the stretcher reached her. She reached for her father's hand.

'Abby, love. I'm sorry.' Max whispered as he tried to lift his arm.

'Take it easy, Dad. You're going to be okay,' she whispered back, and crossed her fingers. At least he was still conscious, but who knew what damage had been done to his head? A severe bruise darkened one side of his face and the eye was swollen shut.

Max's left leg had been put into a splint, and she noted a pressure pad on his thigh. Had the bone pierced the skin? How much blood had he lost before he'd been found?

In the cubicle Sally took baseline obs and compared them with those taken by the paramedics. She quietly showed them to Kieran and the tightening of his mouth made Abby nauseous. Something was going wrong. Panic rose. She gripped the side of the bed with one hand, willing the fear down. She wouldn't help her father by losing control.

'Hey.' Kieran touched her chin.

She met his eyes for a brief moment, saw something almost like love there, but that had to be wishful thinking. She definitely saw real

concern for her and her father. He'd do everything he possibly could for her Dad and that's
all she could ask. 'Thanks.'

Kieran spoke to Sally in such a quiet voice that
Abby didn't hear what he said. But she didn't
have to. She knew what was going on, fully
understood the procedures. Her father was in
the best place possible, receiving the best care
available. She wouldn't have wanted anyone else
looking after him. Kieran was a superb emergency specialist.

So she needed to get her head together. Be
strong. Be strong? Well, if there was one thing
she could do, that was it. If things turned out
really bad for her father then she'd deal with it.
Her throat blocked with unshed tears. *Please
give us a break here. Dad doesn't deserve the
worst. He's already faced a lot of bad things over
the last few years.*

'We're sending Max to Radiology, Abby.'
Kieran spoke beside her. 'The orthopaedic surgeon is on his way as well.'

'His head injury?' She stared at her father's
forehead.

'X-rays will tell us more, but concussion seems
likely.'

The breath she hadn't realised she held whooshed out between her teeth. 'Thank goodness.' If they only had to deal with fractures and blood loss and concussion then things were starting to look up. Very minutely.

How wrong could she be? While the reports about her father's condition continued to improve, it was a different story when she finally got home.

Expecting to find workers busy in the orchard, Abby was shocked to find Fred McCarthy was the only one there. Fred, a semi-retired man who always worked for her father at this time of the year to earn money to pay for his trips overseas, told her he'd been the only worker for weeks now.

The twins joined her soon after Abby learned this devastating news. Steph immediately phoned Andrew to come, and they all crowded around the kitchen table in Max's house to formulate a plan to keep the orchard running. Abby would oversee everything and help with packing the fruit, while the twins and Andrew would pick fruit and see to other jobs as time allowed.

Well after six o'clock Kieran arrived laden with groceries and news of Max.

'The good news is that he hasn't done serious damage to his head. He has a concussion, which will be monitored. The best thing for concussion is to stay in bed and, given his broken leg and three fractured ribs, he isn't going anywhere for a while anyway. The surgery went well. The surgeons had to put a steel pin in his leg.'

The relief around the table was almost palpable. Abby reached for Kieran's hand. 'Thank you for that. We have been trying not to think the worst but it's hard when we didn't know what was going on.'

Kieran dropped a kiss on her cheek and went to cook dinner.

From then on Abby's days were busier than ever. The hours ticked by faster than a speeding train. There was always so much to do. Some varieties of peaches were beginning to come on and needed select picking, packing and getting to the markets. Some trees needed spraying, the grass between the rows needed mowing to make access to the trees easier; boom cannons had to be put in place to scare away the birds. She felt ashamed she hadn't noticed earlier that those things hadn't been done.

Too tied up with Kieran, that had been her problem. Too busy trying to get him to fit into the children's lives to look out for her father. Well, from now on she'd make sure nothing got in the way of doing what was right for all of them. Obviously it was getting too much for her father. From now on she'd stop leaving the children with him so often.

Moving to Dublin would take care of that. But moving to Dublin was no longer an option. She was needed here.

Max saw it differently when she questioned him about the situation on one of her many visits. 'It's time you had a life of your own, my girl. It's not your responsibility to see that I've got everything under control. The fact that orchard workers are in short supply and can demand a lot more money is my problem, not yours.'

'But, Dad, it is my concern. I don't need protecting from anything that's happening with you or the orchard.'

'No, my girl, this is for me to sort out, once I'm out of here. You need to make a life for yourself, one that doesn't involve running around after all of us.'

Abby felt something akin to panic rising in her throat. She loved doing that. It made her feel needed, gave her focus. 'That's me, who I am,' she cried. Never mind that a few days ago she had decided to move to Dublin.

Max reached for her hand. 'No, love. You are a mother first. Then a nurse, my daughter and a sister. But it's time you found your own man to make a home with, to share life with.'

'I'm happy where I am, doing what I do.' Really happy? So happy there was nothing else she wanted in life? Well, she felt safe, at least.

Max studied her. 'Kieran's a good man, love.'

Kieran was a danger to her heart, that's what Kieran was. She might admit to loving him, but that didn't mean she'd risk all to be with him. 'Dad, I suspect you've been hatching plans in your head, but they aren't going to happen. Kieran would be the first to agree with me.'

Now, three days after the accident, Abby stood in her father's office, stretching her back and rolling her head to ease a stiff neck. Where had the day gone? The hours zoomed past when there was so much to do.

The phone rang. 'Hey, how are you doing?' Kieran asked.

'I'm good. Exhausted. But so is everyone, including you.' Kieran had been out at the orchard helping as much as his job allowed. 'I missed you when we came in to see Dad.'

'I was in a meeting with the international interns.' His sigh said it all.

'That bad, huh?' She knew one or two of the interns were hoping to stay on in New Zealand at the end of their contracts with the hospital board.

'Enlightening would be more precise. Hamish also dropped by to tell me that Michael's resigned due to his boy not improving. It's going to be a long time before he's ready to leave Brisbane.'

'How dreadful. We'll miss Michael in the department. He's been an inspirational director. Always takes on the board over financial cuts and staff deployment.' And he'd been good to her when she'd first started in ED, understanding her problems as a single mum.

Kieran was still talking. 'There's some good news. Joey and his mum moved into the women's refuge yesterday.'

'That's great. I am so glad for Joey. Let's hope Dale sticks it out.'

'She sounded pretty determined when I spoke to her. She said to tell you she was sorry about your father's accident.'

'Wow. I wouldn't have thought she'd have noticed anything going on around her.'

Kieran changed the subject. 'Want me to bring Olivia and Seamus out when I'm finished here?'

Charlie had dropped them off in the morning when she'd gone to see Dad. 'That would be great. I know I shouldn't put them in the crèche but how else do I get any work done here?'

'Abby, we all understand. I'll take them up to see Max before we come home.'

Home. If only it was home for Kieran. But that would never happen because he had a damned job in damned Dublin. Blast him. Anyway, her life was here, despite what Dad said. Despite the fact she'd briefly toyed with the idea of following Kieran.

By the time Kieran arrived with the children she'd put all that behind her, if only temporarily. 'Hi, everyone.' She kissed Olivia and hugged Seamus.

Kieran grinned at her. 'Do I get one?'

'Kiss or hug?' The moment the words had left her mouth she wished them back. She could certainly do with one or the other herself. But not the consequences to her heart.

'Both,' Kieran said as he looped his arms around her. Then his lips brushed hers before he withdrew, leaving her shaken and bemused.

And leaving her heart confused. How did he do that to her? She had no control over her mind or body when Kieran touched her. Well, she'd better find some. The children needed baths.

Kieran was putting groceries away. 'I bought chicken. Thought I'd do a leg of lamb for dinner.'

Abby stared at him, her heart melting. What a man. She loved it that he did this, taking a load off her. 'Sounds wonderful. I know the others will be thrilled, too.' Looking out the window she looked for any sign of the twins. Laughter bubbled up when she spotted Steph.

'Look at this. Steph's driving the tractor with the spray unit, and over the other side Charlie's up a ladder, picking peaches.'

Kieran came to stand by her, too close, but she didn't move away. He said, amusement lightening his voice, 'Whatever happened to your glamorous sisters? They seemed to have traded smart suits for old clothes that a scarecrow would be ashamed to wear.'

Abby chuckled. 'They're really putting their hearts into helping.' A yawn caught her.

'They certainly are.' Kieran cleared his throat. 'How much sleep did you get last night?'

She was glad he'd asked, glad that he spent most of his spare time with her. He'd been there for her from the moment he'd learned about Dad's accident. It felt wonderful to have someone at her side when she had all this to deal with.

Another yawn stretched her mouth wide. 'Not a lot,' she admitted. 'Between Seamus waking up three times, me trying to work out what had to be done on the orchard, and wondering how I could get back to work by next Monday, not to mention worrying about Dad, the hours of darkness were riveting. But certainly not filled with sleep.'

'Forget coming back to work on Monday. Sally's already got your shift covered for the whole week.'

She opened her mouth to protest but Kieran

cut in. 'Don't even think it. You're on leave, full stop.'

'Yes, sir. Bossy britches.' She smiled wearily. If only everything else could be fixed so easily.

'Now, how about you see to the kids' baths while I crank up the barbeque? I'll make dinner out on the deck. It's too hot inside.'

'Sounds wonderful. The others will finish in about an hour.' She tapped his shoulder, and when he turned to gaze down at her she almost forgot what she had to say. Almost, but not quite. 'Thanks for everything.' And she kissed him, her lips touching his mouth lightly. She pulled back fast, aware of her need to kiss him thoroughly taking hold. She had to be strong, but as she turned away she saw surprise and warmth in those piercing eyes.

CHAPTER TWELVE

KIERAN leaned back against the railing, observing Abby's family and friends, tiredness dragging at every muscle in his body. Thank goodness for Saturdays. This past week had been exhausting, with the department incredibly busy and his evenings spent out here, in Hope, helping wherever he could.

But happiness overrode his exhaustion. It felt good to have been a part of everything happening in the orchard and in the house. He'd been absorbed into the hustle and bustle as though he belonged. That was the part he liked best. Belonging, however temporarily. No special exceptions were made for him. He'd been treated like all the family.

He smiled, remembering Abby showing him how to use the ride-on mower and then leaving him to the job of mowing the whole orchard.

His eyes had been opened, his brain had finally

assimilated what had been so close under his nose it was a wonder he'd been able to breathe these past weeks. This was where Abby belonged. He couldn't ask her to join him in Dublin for his sake. That would be grossly unfair. If she'd even consider the idea.

He'd watched her taking charge, pulling her family together to keep the orchard running. She'd done it in a way that no one minded, although the twins were obviously used to toeing the line with Abby. They gave her a lot of cheek about her bossiness. And to think she'd previously called him bossy.

'Here, looks like you could do with one of these.' Andrew handed him an icy-cold bottle.

'It's thirsty work, being out in the sun all day,' Kieran acknowledged as he lifted the beer to his lips.

'I reckon this is the best part of the day, with family and friends together for a drink and a meal.'

'Is your family as close as the Brown clan?' Kieran asked.

'Not quite. We don't have an Abby to keep us all together.'

'She's certainly been a tower of strength for

everyone since Max's accident.' She'd amazed
Kieran with her practical approach to the problems facing her once she'd got over her initial
shock of finding there were no workers.

He hadn't forgotten her tears for her father
either, her fear for his life. And how distressed
she'd been on finding out how badly situated
financially this place had become. Another problem Max had kept from her. The past days had
taken it out of Abby more than any of them.
She constantly yawned. Occasionally she'd even
been grumpy.

'From what I've seen and heard, Abby's always
been a strong one,' Andrew added.

'The twins would've managed without her.
People do when there's no choice.' He didn't
want to think of Abby having to be strong for
everyone again. Not on her own, anyway. He
wanted to be there for her, to stand by her, support her, look out for her. From a distance? *How
would that work, boyo?*

Abby pushed the accounts aside and stretched
out in her father's office chair. Another day
nearly done, nothing else needing urgent attention. Everything was working out a lot better

than she'd have believed possible on the day of the accident.

Unless he had a setback, her father would be coming home in two days' time. On the orchard front Andrew had been a surprise. He thrived on all the physical work, had even hinted that he'd like to give up his job as an accountant and get into the orchard business. It would certainly solve a lot of problems for her father if he did.

She could hear him out on the deck chatting with Kieran. The twins were in the kitchen, creating dinner. Scary thought. But it gave her the warm fuzzies the way they'd pulled together with her during this crisis.

Through the window she studied the rows of fruit trees. The afternoon offshore breeze had died away. The air was still and hot. Her favourite time of the day. She should join the others. She would. In a minute. First she wanted a moment to herself.

To think about Kieran.

Now, there was another surprise. Not once had he put his hands up and said no to anything asked of him over the last few days. And he'd been outside his comfort zone many times. That hadn't been the surprise, but more the fact that he'd jumped in to do anything he'd seen that had needing to be done. From cooking meals to changing Seamus's diapers to mowing the orchard.

Her fingers curled tightly. Acting like someone who cared what happened to her family. Like a man who cared what happened to her. She gasped. Did he care for her? Maybe even love her? He hadn't said as much, but hadn't he spent the last few weeks showing her? Kieran had been there for her from the moment Dad had had his accident. Easing her through the horror of seeing Dad smashed up, cooking endless meals for her and her family? If that wasn't showing her, then what was? But did Kieran know that? Did he understand his feelings?

He hadn't shown any characteristics of the playboy he was reputed to be. Sure, he'd been friendly to everyone aged from naught to ninety, not just the females.

She'd wanted to believe the playboy image. It saved her from having to face the truth. Phillip had needed the constant gratification of different women to lift his self-confidence. Another part of Phillip's insecurities meant that he continuously put her down, told her she was unattractive, and that she should've been grateful he'd wanted to marry her. He'd shouted at her that no one else would as she'd tossed her bags into her car the day she'd left him.

Kieran had proved him wrong. He'd been loyal to her, helped her out when no one else had even thought to offer a hand. The reputation her brother had warned her about years ago seemed to be a thing of the past. Kieran had probably dated a lot of different women because of his aversion to settling down. And that, she knew, came from his belief that he wouldn't be a good husband or father. He mightn't have had a good role model for either of those roles but somewhere in his life he'd learned anyway. Or was it just an intrinsic part of his make-up to be caring and loving and loyal?

Olivia bounced into the office, Seamus toddling along behind. 'Abby, come and see what I've done for you.'

'You've done something for me?' Abby leaned forward and hugged Olivia to her. The kids. Where would she be without them? She loved them so much.

She loved Kieran so much. And she'd have to learn to live without him being around.

Olivia squirmed in her arms. 'You were sad so I drawed some flowers.'

'Flowers? For me? Sweetheart, that's lovely. Where is this picture?'

'Seamus scribbled on one flower. Bad boy.' Olivia grabbed her hand and tugged her out to the hall, where she stopped and pointed proudly. 'See? Aren't they pretty?'

Abby gaped. At the wall. The bottom half was covered in vividly coloured shapes. Every colour under the rainbow. Every colour out of Olivia's indelible pen set. 'Oh, my goodness.'

'You like the flowers, Abby?'

Abby sank back against the opposite wall, slid down onto her haunches. 'They're beautiful but...' What was Dad going to say? He'd finished painting the interior of the house only a couple of months ago. There wouldn't be time to repaint before he got home. 'Olivia, darling, why didn't you ask me for some paper to draw on?'

'You were busy.'

She couldn't argue with that.

Seamus toddled up with a marker pen in his hand, ready to add further to the artistic display.

Abby grabbed his hand, gently removed the pen. 'No, Seamus.'

She blinked back sudden tears. Another problem. More work to be done. It seemed never-ending.

'Hey, what's going on?' Kieran stopped in the middle of the hall, his mouth dropping open as he took in the newly redecorated wall. 'Oh, blimey.'

'I drawed flowers to make Abby happy.'

'So I see.' Kieran turned to peer down at Abby, his lips twitching.

'Don't you dare laugh.' Two big tears rolled over her cheekbones.

He sank down to sit beside her, his shoulder touching hers. 'Hard not to, to be sure.' His mouth began stretching into a grin, and laughter threatened. 'This is the ultimate in gifts. A permanent drawing to cheer you up whenever you feel down.'

'"Permanent" being the operative word.' She batted his thigh with the back of her hand. 'It's not funny.' But her tears stopped.

'Olivia, go and find Abby a box of tissues, please.' Kieran twisted round to look at Abby, her face so woebegone he wanted to hug her to him and make everything right for her. Instead, he kissed each salty cheek before asking, 'How do we find out what paint Max used in here?'

'There's probably a tin in the shed. He never throws them out.' She was shaking her head. 'I don't believe this.'

'If you're right and there's still paint around, we'll have the problem fixed in no time. Maybe not today, but soon.'

'You're not here for much longer.' Her bottom lip quivered.

'It won't take long to fix this. I'll do it after work one night. Maybe tomorrow before Max comes home. I think that would be best.' Max might not see the funny side of Olivia's home-improvement idea. There again, the man was fairly relaxed about his grandchildren so he might.

'You can paint?' Those delectable lips twitched. 'As in with a roller and wide brush?'

'Can't be too hard. I learned to drive that ride-on mower, didn't I?' He winked.

Now she did an eye-roll. 'Soon you'll be telling people you're a handyman.'

Olivia pressed a tissue box onto Abby's lap. 'A

tissue, a tissue, I fall down.' Which she promptly did, giggling as she rolled all over the floor.

'Okay, Olivia, Seamus. Pens, please.' Kieran began to collect the numerous colouring pens.

Olivia began helping. Seamus picked one up and brought it to Abby.

'Give it to Daddy.' Abby blew her nose and wiped her eyes.

'Daddy.' Seamus handed Kieran the pen.

The pen dropped through Kieran's lifeless fingers. 'What?' He stared at Seamus. His throat ached, his ears hurt, his eyes watered. 'What?' he croaked again.

'Daddy.' Seamus picked the pen up and stood looking from Kieran to Abby and back. Almost as though he wasn't sure which one of them was Daddy.

Kieran asked, 'Did I hear right?'

Abby looked as stunned as he felt. Her mouth opened but nothing came out. Was she disappointed? Hurt even? She had every right to be. She'd done the hard yards with Seamus, not him. But he only saw pride in her eyes.

Kieran touched her shoulder, ran his finger down her cheek. His voice sounded scratchy when he spoke. 'That's amazing. I can't believe

I heard Seamus speak his first clear word. But it was the wrong word.'

How did she really feel about this? Seamus's first word. It should've been 'Mummy'. He looked closer, saw nothing but joy in her face. She had to the most generous person he had ever been lucky enough to meet. 'Abby?'

Ripping another handful of tissues from the box, she dabbed at her tears. 'That's the most beautiful thing I've heard in for ever.'

'Isn't it?' Now his smile grew, stretching his mouth wide. 'Unbelievable.'

Seamus, unaware of the turmoil he'd caused, tossed the pen on Abby's lap and went in search of another one. Kieran reached for him, lifted him into his arms and held him close. 'Say it again.'

But Seamus had tired of that game. He stared up at Kieran, chuckling and banging his hands on his father's chest. A chest that was about to break wide open with love. Seamus had just done what he'd believed impossible. His son had shown him love was within reach, was simple if he opened up to it.

One little word. A huge word. Daddy. He was a daddy. His son had told him so. His head banged against the wall behind him and he closed his eyes, shutting the moment in. Then snapped them open again, looking at Abby. This was her moment, too. The first time her son had spoken something comprehensible.

'It should've been "Mummy".' He repeated it quietly but with feeling. He meant it. He'd stolen her moment.

'That doesn't matter. Truly. I'm just thankful I heard it. It's so special.'

'It's magical.' He reached a hand to her and she took it, wrapping her fingers around his.

She nodded. 'The firsts are always the best.'

She never gave up telling him what he might be missing out on when he left. He smiled at her. 'You're wonderful, you know that?'

He saw her swallow before she looked away from him. Didn't she believe him? She had to. He meant it. With all his body. With everything he had. With his heart.

This wasn't about the children. This was about Abby. About the two of them. About the life they could make together. The life he wanted to make with her.

Emotion swamped him as he looked at the

woman who'd snagged his heart. Love suffused him. Fear gripped him.

He couldn't leave.

Not Abby or the children.

Not now or ever. This was where he belonged. Not in some large hospital on the other side of the world where his only claim to life was being a very good emergency specialist. No, he was meant to be a father. To Seamus and Olivia.

But more importantly he could never, ever leave Abby. He needed her. He had so much to give her.

Seamus wriggled out of his arms and toddled towards another pen, which he picked up and handed to Abby, triumph lighting up his eyes.

Abby took it, placing a light kiss on her son's forehead. 'Thank you, darling. You clever boy, you.'

Kieran gulped, swallowed, breathed deep. And reached for Abby's hand. 'Abby, I'm not leaving.'

'Of course not. The twins are cooking dinner.'

His fingers took her chin, turned her head so he could look deep into those hazel orbs. 'No, Abby, you don't understand. This isn't about dinner or about tomorrow or the next day. I'm not leaving. I'm staying on in Nelson. I'll apply for Michael's job, and if I don't get that I'll find something else. I can't go away. I—'

She placed her forefinger over his lips. Her mouth spread into a smile, growing wider as he watched. 'You're staying.'

'Yeah, I'm staying.'

Abby was still smiling when, five weeks later, the plane lifted off from Nelson on the first leg of their trip. Beside her Kieran groaned, and his hand gripped hers even harder.

'At this rate every bone in my hand will be broken by the time we get to Dublin.' At least it wasn't her left hand, with the dazzling emerald in its simple gold setting winking at her from her ring finger.

Kieran tried to relax his hold. 'Sorry, sweetheart. But I hate flying. Intensely.'

Sweetheart. The endearment still filled her with warmth every time she heard it, and that was often. 'Maybe we should've stayed at home and you could've organised selling your apartment, packing up the furniture and all those other things by phone and email.'

'You have no idea how tempting that was. But

there are some things I have to be present to do. Like saying goodbye to all my staff, and to my boss, the guy who insisted I do some time away from Dublin before I started at Mercy Hospital.' He chuckled. 'Ethel told me I'd have a beautiful young woman to accompany me on this trip.'

'Ethel?'

'A very intuitive old lady who sat by me for the flight into Nelson. Perhaps I should look her up and invite her to the wedding.'

'Go on. What's one more person?' The wedding numbers were growing by the day. The wedding. Her stomach gave an excited squeeze. She still couldn't quite believe it. She and Kieran getting married had seemed such a remote possibility that there were moments when she thought she must be dreaming.

'I'll call Charlie about it.' She smiled widely.

Charlie had taken over organising the wedding while they were away. Her organisational skills were surprisingly formidable. Had she learned that from her older sister?

Kieran ran a finger down her cheeks, wiping the lines left by tears from when she'd hugged her kids one last time at the airport. 'They'll be fine with Steph.'

'I know.' They'd only be gone for fourteen days but she'd never been apart from them for more than a day at a time. Seamus was too young to understand and seemed more interested in watching the planes taking off and landing. But Olivia had clung to her, crying and wanting to make sure Abby would come back. 'Not like Mummy,' she'd wailed. That's when Abby had very nearly cancelled her flight.

'Olivia will be fine the moment you've gone through the gate,' Steph, who was looking after the children while they were away, had assured her. 'You can phone her every night. Just go and enjoy yourselves. It is your honeymoon.'

Abby leaned over to kiss Kieran. 'Who has a honeymoon before the wedding?'

'People who can't wait for all the red tape regarding a certain Irishman and his wedding being dealt with. People who can't wait to be together. People who love each other so much it hurts.'

'People like us.'

'Yeah, people like us.' And he leaned in to

kiss her. Not a peck on the cheek or chin, but a full-blown husband-to-be kiss.

Under his lips Abby grinned. Hopefully he'd forgotten they were thousands of feet up in the air.

* * * * *

Mills & Boon® Large Print
Medical

October

TAMING DR TEMPEST	Meredith Webber
THE DOCTOR AND THE DEBUTANTE	Anne Fraser
THE HONOURABLE MAVERICK	Alison Roberts
THE UNSUNG HERO	Alison Roberts
ST PIRAN'S: THE FIREMAN AND NURSE LOVEDAY	Kate Hardy
FROM BROODING BOSS TO ADORING DAD	Dianne Drake

November

HER LITTLE SECRET	Carol Marinelli
THE DOCTOR'S DAMSEL IN DISTRESS	Janice Lynn
THE TAMING OF DR ALEX DRAYCOTT	Joanna Neil
THE MAN BEHIND THE BADGE	Sharon Archer
ST PIRAN'S: TINY MIRACLE TWINS	Maggie Kingsley
MAVERICK IN THE ER	Jessica Matthews

December

FLIRTING WITH THE SOCIETY DOCTOR	Janice Lynn
WHEN ONE NIGHT ISN'T ENOUGH	Wendy S. Marcus
MELTING THE ARGENTINE DOCTOR'S HEART	Meredith Webber
SMALL TOWN MARRIAGE MIRACLE	Jennifer Taylor
ST PIRAN'S: PRINCE ON THE CHILDREN'S WARD	Sarah Morgan
HARRY ST CLAIR: ROGUE OR DOCTOR?	Fiona McArthur

Mills & Boon® Large Print Medical

January

THE PLAYBOY OF HARLEY STREET	Anne Fraser
DOCTOR ON THE RED CARPET	Anne Fraser
JUST ONE LAST NIGHT…	Amy Andrews
SUDDENLY SINGLE SOPHIE	Leonie Knight
THE DOCTOR & THE RUNAWAY HEIRESS	Marion Lennox
THE SURGEON SHE NEVER FORGOT	Melanie Milburne

February

CAREER GIRL IN THE COUNTRY	Fiona Lowe
THE DOCTOR'S REASON TO STAY	Dianne Drake
WEDDING ON THE BABY WARD	Lucy Clark
SPECIAL CARE BABY MIRACLE	Lucy Clark
THE TORTURED REBEL	Alison Roberts
DATING DR DELICIOUS	Laura Iding

March

CORT MASON – DR DELECTABLE	Carol Marinelli
SURVIVAL GUIDE TO DATING YOUR BOSS	Fiona McArthur
RETURN OF THE MAVERICK	Sue MacKay
IT STARTED WITH A PREGNANCY	Scarlet Wilson
ITALIAN DOCTOR, NO STRINGS ATTACHED	Kate Hardy
MIRACLE TIMES TWO	Josie Metcalfe